Living Life
Backwards

Peter Wells

NARRATUS
PDMI PUBLISHING, LLC
Albertville, Alabama USA

PDMI Publishing, LLC
P.O. Box 56
Albertville, Alabama, U.S.A 35950.
www.pdmipublishing.com

Ordering Information: Quantity sales and special discounts are available on quantity purchases by corporations, associations, and others. For details, contact the publisher at the address above. Orders by U.S. trade bookstores and wholesalers. Please contact PDMI Publishing, LLC: Tel: (855) 782-5474; Fax: (256) 485-4697 or visit the Ingram Catalog at ipage.ingramcontent.com.

Printed in the United States of America.

Printing History: First Edition, First Printing, February 2014.

1 2 3 4 5

ISBN-10: 1940812542; ISBN-13: 978-1-940812-54-0; Library of Congress Control Number: 2014932624

Narratus logo is a ® registered trademark of PDMI Publishing, LLC.

Cover Illustration by: Elizabeth Mueller; Cover Design by: TC McKinney; Interior Format by: Nessa Arcamenel; Edited by: Stacey Brewer

PDMI Publishing, LLC is a BBB Accredited Member and Proud IBPA Member.

Our Printers at PDMI use acid-free, interior paper stock that is supplied by an (SFI®), (FSC®), and (PEFC®) certified provider.

PUBLISHER'S NOTE

Author Website: www.countingducks.wordpress.com

For Tom whose support and encouragement have been unfailing.

☆

For Nadeema who made everything possible.

☆

For my daughters Julia, Philippa and Lilly, because what would I
have without them.

Chapter One

I am done with intimacy. The chaos is destructive. No identity is safe from it, at least not mine. Whether I was drowning because my life with Katie had removed me from the familiar or because I existed in a world free of all emotional warmth and just the promise of a touch made me lose my sanity I cannot say. Perhaps you will be the judge of that.

In those heady, early days of marriage, I would have lived anywhere just to have my wife and her world in my sight and arms, so I moved my life to hers. I found employment as a local book keeper in the seaside town where her mother and father lived, as did much of her extended family. Of all these relatives, she was closest to the Potts family, David and Margaret, who were her aunt and uncle. David Potts was a man of infinite patience who kept a discrete distance from real life. His electricity was generated by a series of self-built windmills spread around his farm and painted in various colours, and his dress sense was individual and flamboyant. He seemed unworldly in every matter but one: the pricing of vegetables. On this subject alone he demonstrated normal levels of acumen. I know, I kept the books for his smallholding.

Katie's principle connection with the family was through her young cousin, Misty. I can never say her name without emotion.

I was hauled along in the slipstream of Katie's social

activities. We were ten and twelve years older than Misty, for whom Katie had babysat as a young adult. She had watched Misty grow, and then leave for college and return. Katie was her mentor, her shaper, and her guide, and for much of Misty's early youth, Katie's influence might have been regarded as shallow but not dangerous. I'm speculating here. I was not present myself at that time, but possibly some change in Katie's life changed her way with Misty – a development to which I might have contributed.

Katie had a physical beauty and strength of will which had torn me from my previous path and roots and placed me here, somewhere out of my depths. I had followed her willingly for reasons I will make clear. Her gaze, once softened by interest, now moved remorselessly from objects to situations, either wishing for one or longing for the other. My job was to smile and make it possible. Despite my best endeavours, I felt my standing in her eyes had gradually dwindled. Contempt sometimes made itself known in the flick of her head or the passing of attention.

I remember some visitor remarking, in the midst of some social gathering, "You're rather put upon," as they stared directly into my eyes.

"It's a possibility," I said.

I kept my dreams to myself and my actions to a minimum. I discovered having a reputation for being boring has advantages. On the weekends, I often drove my wife to some occasion, or she went off to appointments at hair or nail salons, and I used the time provided by her absence to live a life of imagination.

If you are not sure you love someone, find something in them to love. It may see you through.

When we first met she had, or so I thought, loved or admired me for reasons of reliability and an ability to entertain. After a few bruising romantic encounters, she was happy to settle for me. For someone stable who could be relied upon. I felt honoured. She called me her harbour. I mistook her approval for admiration and now I was paying the price of my error. Such is life.

Recently, thoughts of Misty threatened to engulf me. It was

important to ensure that an interest did not threaten what I most valued: my detachment. It was important, but it was not easy.

So why did Katie stay with me, and I with her? I ask that question, and my answers keep on changing. For me, Katie was a form of entertainment, but more importantly, she was the door through which I gained access to her family and community. In them I experienced the nearest thing to a home I had ever known.

My father was a wealthy man, although mean and sparing in the way he helped his only son, but in time and with a fair wind, he breathed his last and would finally allow my wife the lifestyle for which she hungered. She never said that, but she sometimes, in looser and more intimate moments, pointed out some holiday or piece of furniture as if to say. "We'll enjoy that. We'll have that," and other expressions of deferred excitement. Apart from that, I had a reputation for patience which she tested at her leisure and the ability to be predictable.

For Misty, as far as I knew, I was attached to Katie. She accepted my presence as unremarkable It was a compliment of a kind. I'd earned a level of trust, and I would live with that. For the Potts family as a whole, I was the man in a suit, their ambassador to common sense. I had sat – a recorder of sorts – through the later part of their family history. David Potts, now bald but wearing his remaining hair over-long and sporting Lennon glasses, was not a windbag but made pronouncements without context.

"Literal men will never learn the truth," is one I remember.

Time permitting, he would sit on his hill and sniff out the messages held within weather patterns and the passing clouds – some mystic resonance for his sense alone. Rain did not deter him, or thunder, or the parching heat. He was a man on a mission, a fanatic with a placid manner who would not be deterred. Only his wife understood this, as far as I know.

Much of what I tell you, I learnt from my place in the background – someone who happened to be there and might be useful. Around the time of which I speak 'Lemongrass,' some character from the internet, had become a topic of conversation between the girls. Katie, because she loved romance as long as it was not personal and Misty because, despite her history, still had moments when she dreamed of some man walking through the screen to save her.

Speaking of 'Lemongrass' to a group of friends, Misty said, "He's a poet and so, you know... connected." They all sighed. Such sensitivity!

It was the first time I heard the name.

As they talked, I read the paper as if their conversation held no interest. The secret of Misty's fascination for me was in the emotional wilderness in which I found myself; that is my excuse. It made me vulnerable to the slightest sign of interest, and sometimes she gave me that. Morsels really, fragments at best, but still painfully nourishing to a soul as desperate as mine.

"Oh, Bill, you're a dear," and, "You're so lucky to have him, Kate," said while lightly brushing my arm could take on fresh significance when viewed with desperation. She leaned forward when speaking, "You understand me don't you, Bill. Bill always knows." Everything she said appeared to be in confidence and for your ears alone. That, somehow, she believed only you would grasp the whole significance. Compliments I found too hard to resist.

On matters of common sense, I was often consulted by her father, who sneered at the ownership of most possessions, but was strangely vulnerable to any discussion concerning Misty. He had not confronted the idea that one day she might not be near at hand. Travel held little interest to him. He voyaged by means of imagination only. Yes, he called her 'Misty' or 'Sunshine' or 'Lovely' depending on his mood, but sometimes, when rhapsodic emotions gripped him, he would say her full name: Misty Margaret Potts. It was clear it held a magic for him that could not be tampered with. Misty – deep and facile, whimsical and firm – loved her Dad and could not wound him. For him, she would always be the cherub running through his fields with a garland of flowers in her hair. It was her sacred trust. Most of the bonds which hold us are intangible. We know that to our cost.

I remember my first sighting of Misty, when I was still

largely a stranger to her circle, at a gathering to mark her start at teachers training college and her mother's birthday. "Two for the price of one," as someone said. I was not yet married to Katie but was still dazzled by what I saw as her social brilliance and especially by the lovely family and close community she enjoyed in her home town. Apart from myself, everyone knew each other, and even I, the new kid on the block, was made warmly welcome. I had rescued Katie from disaster, in some way, and after her initial suspicions, she had adopted me as a sort of local hero who had turned her life around and, as such, been welcomed by her family.

It seeped out through various indiscretions that not all Katie's previous companions had been as trustworthy as her parents would like, and I was regarded as being a surprisingly and refreshingly stable and boring addition to her circle. I had met a few of the locals, but not the Potts, so this was a significant moment. As I mingled with the party making small talk, a girl walked out of the house, looked around her, and then went up to Mr Potts, as I then called him, and kissed him on the cheek. To say she was attractive does not capture the quality of intoxication I experienced on seeing her, but remember, I was being feted as the new and sober beau of her cousin, and as such, I could admit no interest.

When we were finally introduced, I kept my expression as blank as possible but, even at our initial meeting, there was something knowing and even intimate about her, as if she sensed a special connection. I later learnt, from observation that she did that with most men, and how she had remained single was not easy to understand. In hindsight, I think she liked to tease but not to play. She lived at home in a small community with her parents who were over-protective, or I thought so. It was not easy to remain impassive. Clearly, I wanted to know anything I could about her but could show no interest. Riding one horse while admiring another is no easy task – I knew that already – but knowing and understanding are two different things as I learnt to my cost.

The only thing I discovered, apart from her having had no serious boyfriends, was she liked cats, dogs, and chickens. That was all I learnt.

Am I revealing too much of my feelings? That was always my concern from the moment I met her. My interest and focus must remain with Katie whose interest in me was still exciting enough for me to suppress any doubts I had about any depth of commitment. Being with one and glancing at the other was a sure way to lose both. Even I understood that, and to Misty I was just a friend of Katie's, I was sure. That was an opinion I held onto for the coming years. What I knew was that this community, and the spirit within in it, were like nothing I had ever experienced and to be part of it was like a miraculous home coming and something I would never put at risk.

In time Katie and I married because the lady was entertaining and seemed to need me, and the community was intoxicating to a man who had never had a home or family of any warmth apart from one aunt with whom visits were infrequent.

Don't call me cold-hearted or tactical. There was more to it than that. Katie truly was involving, if that is the word, and her whole family made me feel one of them in a way I had never experienced anywhere else and especially with my own father. I loved my wife, of course, in my own way, but what I loved most deeply was being part of something, of finally belonging in a place I might call home. Misty was largely absent at the beginning as she pursued her career in college, so thoughts of her were forgotten – or should I say latent – and Katie and I formed a predictable alliance based on shared objectives or some such nonsense. In hindsight, I am no longer sure.

In time, Misty returned to the village and was to start that autumn as an assistant in the village school.

~2~

Broccoli Romanesco is a hybrid of broccoli and cauliflower and lime green in colour. It requires an even temperature and consistent water supply in a good, organic soil to thrive. David

Potts knew this because he grew rare vegetables. He grew a decent number of them and sent them to market up in the city where the *cognoscenti* could sample them and dream of a simpler, less complicated life. While these uncomplaining plants lived within his greenhouse they were his children, his charges. Everything he did was in detail and for their benefit. He was not a broad brush man. For him, every sentence contained the heart of the book, every leaf the tree, and every courtesy the character. His most urgent conversations were with himself, but in his dealings with others he was benign.

His wife Margaret was a decent, round, and caring women who lived with his introspection and somehow saw his eccentricities as a celebration of the individual. She was one of those beings who would let you be as you are as long it didn't harm or damage anyone. These people are rare but do exist. That they should have found each other was one of nature's wonders but also left them unschooled in any dealings with the darker forces of man or circumstance. To date at least.

That is where I came in. I was there as a middle man between their home and business life, and it was a role I enjoyed. Sometimes at breakfast, as he read some book on his current obsession, she might throw a slice of toast at him to gain his attention but otherwise pretty much let him be as he did her. It was not a barren relationship but merely tolerant. The secret's in the look. Between loving couples, tenderness spills out of the eyes at the oddest moment. It is the hallmark of a contented home.

Thus with him in his greenhouses or striding in his fields and her inside tending to her home or quilting for her own pleasure, they were ever never alone. The heart of companionship is being understood, and this they had. They were two slightly un-socialised people who had found a way to deal with the world by supplying a niche foodstuff at no social cost to themselves. Freed from the need to be overly manicured, they had become slowly, quietly, gently odder over the years. Misty was their only child and thus beyond precious. She was always sweet and gentle in their opinion and with her own brand of beauty. That was their belief.

Whatever our plan or nature, children force the most isolated of us to deal with society at large, and this had been the case with Misty. At school, at parties, or with groups of gossiping and uncertain adolescents she had brought the world, village-sized, to their door. Treaties were made through the medium of Mrs. Potts' home-made lemonade or games of hide and seek in the fields behind their house. Their tolerance made them friends. As the children grew older, temptation made its presence known but in a small community where everyone and everything were familiar, the cost of straying towards destructive behaviour was high. Doors were not locked.

When Misty finally returned from college, her unguarded trust had been somewhat damaged, in a manner yet unknown, by some city boy or boys who had no knowledge of rare vegetables. Who thought, perhaps, that winning was the secret of life, and so it might be, but not for the losers or less cynical. For people like Misty, college had proved a tempering experience. Back home and with a summer to enjoy, she sought to heal her bruises secret within herself.

Her parents had little knowledge of conflict or what they regarded as poor behaviour and practised a tolerance based on their own gentle approach to life, the benefits of living in a small and stable community. They were not naïve, but that was different to having to confront unschooled lust or recklessness in their own back yard. The boys back home were known and trusted. Those with a looser grip on their appetites were given a wider birth, at least by Misty and her parents and those they knew. City life was beyond their experience and they were disturbed by the effect wrought on Misty by her exposure to it: nothing terrible as such, but now she seemed slightly more wary and less trusting. Perhaps more nervy, and this disturbed them. Through no fault of her own, she was more than averagely pretty, and this had made her a prize for those not necessarily interested in marriage. She had kept her dignity and modesty intact but at some cost to her peace of mind. This was obvious to her parents, and they sought to ease the experience from her memory. Never an easy task.

On Saturday's, Katie would often vanish on a range of appointments centred round hair and nail care with the odd head or foot massage thrown in.

"I'm so stressed," she said staring at me. "Why are you so difficult?"

I would reply with something like, "I think it's a design problem," and she would give me a charged stare before leaving the room. Despite myself, there was a vulnerable quality about her vanity, which brought out the protective in me. Despite herself, I think it was my patience which kept her by my side apart from my father's money, of course, and my standing with her family.

Through her, even by accident, I had met a community I loved and people with whom a good and unstated friendship was possible. The town was low on self-confessed high achievers and survived mainly on the fishing industry, tourism, and the odd farm around the outskirts. I felt at home there, and the fact that I wanted no more than this was another source of irritation in the heart of my beloved. To be fair to me, and who else would be, she was someone who would find the irritating in any one or thing, so I had not been singled out in that regard. What she had always liked, before she met me, was excitement and change, which was hard to find in a place largely governed by the tides. She was held there by the demands of her mother. A woman blessed with finely tuned nerves.

Once alone, I used to wander out and sniff the air. Regularly, I would venture up to the green houses where David Potts could be found tending to and talking with his patient vegetables in his own slightly eccentric manner.

"Now don't be greedy. You know it's not good for you," he might say out loud to some non-committal buds lying in their fertile tray. "Oh, hello, Bill. Have you been to the house yet?"

He always asked that in case I was the bearer of coffee, but today I had just wandered straight in. In theory, I would be talking about the month's turnover, tax returns, or other subjects of pleasing neutrality, but sometimes he might move nearer a topic of more pressing concern then, without explanation, he switched his conversation back to his plants and the cycles of the moon or to anything which drew his mind away from the danger he sensed in anything impulsive.

He wanted me to talk to Misty about some internet dating craze she and Katie had got caught up with, which presented its own difficulties: ignoring my feelings for the moment. The central problem was that the internet dating idea had been Katie's in the first place, and she wanted Misty to have what she thought she longed for: adventure and the open road, a life slightly above the ordinary, a man less clumsy and unschooled than the boys the village could provide. Whatever Misty's private feelings, Katie was always warning her off settling for some 'cloth-eared' local boy, and the world seemed as good a place to start as any.

David Potts raised his eyes directly to mine, and in them I saw something unusual: concern. There is no happiness which does not censor much of what is possible in life, and now his child was placing his undemanding calm in the path of a world he had always sought to ignore.

Sometimes in a glance over recent months, I got the sense that he suspected my feelings for Misty had grown above the ordinary, but he thought he understood me. He felt, whatever my feelings, that I believed in cherishing without possessing. It was a subtlety of outlook which we both enjoyed discussing, though detachment, I had discovered, was painful in itself, and this – watching a figure we both loved in different ways, however secretly, get involved in a situation for which she had no training – was beyond hard. We both knew that without Katie this would never have happened.

Without Katie lying with her on her bed saying, "What about him?" and, "He looks nice," Misty's natural reticence would have prevented the presence of a danger we both feared.

But what could we do? We knew much more what not to say, than what to say. In the world of accounts or vegetable growing there is little activity which can be called impulsive. Neither of us was trained to deal with the consequences of rash behaviour, and we sought no dealings with it.

Katie, who most probably had been bored from the moment of her birth, felt quite differently about the matter. She craved excitement and travel and chatter, but her circumstances denied her the experience.

Yes, when first we met, all she had wanted to do was come home, and it was one of the stipulations for our marriage, but that was because she, too, had been bruised by the experience of surviving in a city with people who sought to use her for their own entertainment. For a time, at least, she had grown tired of city life and longed for a safe return to the dependable adventures and imaginings of her mother. I must have seemed a reliable companion for that venture.

Forgetting her original stipulations she often railed against me, "Why aren't you more ambitious? Is this all you want? I thought you were a man with dreams."

Strangely, reminding her of what she had demanded before accepting my proposal, or that she chose me because I did not seem to be a man of dreams, never seemed to silence her. She was like a fly trapped by a pane of glass and hungering for the world outside. In Misty, she had someone who would be as she now wished to be. Who would venture fearlessly forth and experience the exotic. Misty, even with her recent and bruising experience of the city, was somehow in thrall to Katie and was swept along by her excitement.

~3~

I have heard that many of the most interesting conversations you have are with yourself. It was certainly true for me. In the eyes of my wife, it sometimes appeared, I was an unfinished and irritating being. That had soon become her common stance. Although there was also the sense that this informed her attitude to life in general, which she saw as standing between her and her constantly changing objectives. Her irritation and admiration where equally charged by the fact that I was quite well received by most who knew us and thus the subject of affection and some interest.

"Try living with him," she often said. "Bill just walks around looking for things to knock over," and other expressions of a patience worn thin by experience. On the other hand, I was liked by her father, and even her mother always stared at me with that bright electric smile which unsettles all but the sleepiest of men.

I got through the day and sometimes night by refining my ideas. I had grown to love the concept of the causeless cause, of forgotten qualities like chivalry and selflessness. I was always refining my concept about 'the beauty of a moment' as if it were a work of art sculpted in breath. That if I could recognise my growing and unsettling love for Misty, but deflect its dangerous implications by wrapping it in some medieval idealism, it might make the whole experience bearable and possibly beautiful. It was a nicety appreciated by me, although hard to convey to those around me, were I to be brave or stupid enough to do so. For them, I persisted in my policy of good manners without agenda, patience without benefit, and the odd self-deprecating story. It got me by. It kept me out of harm's way and allowed me the freedom to have those thoughts I should not have.

I recognised that my inner and outer life were growing more and more separate from each other and that was a concern. I don't mean concern, of course. That is too balanced, but you may follow me. I saw the danger of it. That's what it was. I was, at one and the same time, drawn to the smooth beautiful coolness of the water I saw from my vantage point in this emotional desert and aware of the price to be paid by those who trespass onto private grounds to drink it. I must offer what I felt up to the fates, to the history of man, and the beauty of emotions unrequited. I must do anything but act on it. To do that would be to lose everything I had worked so hard to maintain. To invite ridicule and shame in unbearable quantities and hurt the feelings of people whose values I regarded as one of the wonders of nature. I could not contemplate that.

Sometimes on these walks of reflection, I would move along the breakwater – about a mile long – and sit on the end of it with nothing but the sea before me and the thin outline of another town on the opposite side of the bay. I would watch the trawler's plough through the water toward some unspecified fishing ground. I loved the sea and the trawlers: the sea, for its impersonal moods and strengths, and the trawlers for the fact that everything on them had a function. Nothing in or about them was there for vanity or comfort. It was there for economy of action and the need to survive whatever the weather threw at it. This stripped down quality, almost like the floating and mechanical embodiment of a monk – purpose without vanity – was inspiring to me. This is how I recharged myself: in the recognition of basic needs and life forces, in the power of the impersonal to challenge us all.

Whatever the dangers and threats imposed by such an environment, it was less frightening and apocalyptic than giving into my personal feelings. I had my daydreams, and what man does not, even in the presence of a pretty girl, but I knew the dangers of following them. I had learnt painful lessons, and I had no wish to repeat them. I swore to myself that I would be as the tides: dependable and unmoved by whims.

Katie's mother and father were a bit like me and Katie, but somewhat higher up the food chain. Her father ran the garage in the town and was a self-contained and practical man who was relied on to do the job and not over charge for his services. His hands were often oily and his shirts were soiled by his habit of using them as a cloth. On the one hand, they had prosperity and comfort, but on the other hand, there was no style. You know what I mean. None of those little details which make a household stand out from its neighbours, and Mrs. Ballard, the name by which I stilled called Katie's mother, was a women obsessed by detail and bored by events.

"Oh, Geoffrey," she might say, "Why couldn't I marry a man who might buy me flowers once in a while," and then shoot me a conspiratorial glance for all to see. Of course, I never brought flowers either, although I loved to see them in the ground.

Grumbling at low volume was their normality. Mother and daughter now joyously celebrating a common burden: men with no imagination. If only we gave them free rein, what colours there would be, what parties and music and joy. This is what they both said, but the irony was that, in Katie's case, getting ready for a party was nearly all the fun.

Moving towards me in a range of frocks and saying, "What about this?"

To which I always replied "Beautiful."

And she would reply, "Everything is beautiful to you. Everything is amazing. It's so boring," and then she'd flounce off only to return five minutes later with some fresh garment or piece of jewellery.

At last, we'd leave the house for whatever event it was. As soon as possible, just beyond the point where it was not outwardly rude to do so, she'd suggest we go home. It was something she was noted for. My enjoyment was never a factor. In company she was acting the jolly girl, and acting always tires you in the end. Apart from me, she liked material distractions and Misty – her special exception. The girl who would, on her behalf, explore the world without anxiety. Katie would make it happen, and damn the man who suggested such a thing was folly.

Geoff, as he was more commonly known, always smiled at me quietly, and on rare occasions might suggest we "go across the road" which meant a pint but never more than three. For the controlling woman, nothing is more disturbing than the normally pliant male freed from his inhibitions by alcohol. To watch him suddenly letting thoughts and observations best left unsaid out into the open.

Once or twice I had spoken with alcohol fuelled recklessness, which took no account of the punishments bound to come when euphoria had left the room. Once or twice I had 'forgotten myself' and brought to life that rhapsodic carefree and eccentric student I used to be and let rip with a range of impersonations and jokes which, at the time, appeared to amuse the company.

Katie's face, when I was sober enough to see it, was not an uplifting sight.

"I do not love you at this moment," she once said. "You made a fool of yourself and me, and why do you have to hug everybody? You just make them cringe."

I found it best not to reply. So on my drinks with her father and in normal events, I watched myself. A man who lives internally and moves through life as if in a tank cannot afford to jump out and let his thoughts run naked for all to see. It would be guaranteed oblivion. And yet those thoughts, which I offered up with increasing fervour to the sky above, longed to speak. Just to see the light of day and affirm the presence of the beautiful in my increasingly airless life.

Sometimes, her mother and father would come to ours or we would go to them. Often when they did, the girls would exclaim about a new set of cushions or share a longing for new cutlery, and the men would be delighted that their chatter had removed us from the need to converse, but we were never fooled. There was nothing stupid about Katie. In the defence of her own circumstances or status she was more than alert and her job as a letting agent kept her involved with the reality of day to day commerce in a way which was not evident from her evening conversation. Her mother had never really worked after Katie was born, and Katie was her Misty, if you follow me.

Sometimes, I reflected that the loudest voice in the room is seldom the wisest, but I kept that observation to myself. For a material girl there is nothing more irritating than a husband who is poor or unambitious, apart from when he's right. That is unforgivable.

Chapter Two

Most of us are not intentionally evil or destructive. That opinion might be marked by an innocence I protect myself with. That being said, most of us cause harm to others as a result of carelessness, selfishness, or acts of self-absorption. That was probably the case with Bernard. As he moved through his life, he threw the litter of his mind and imagination overboard allowing it to pollute other's lives, and in the process destroyed his marriage and his peace of mind. The place he found himself in was the result of appetites unchecked and not the desire to harm. I've always thought that anyway.

Perhaps you might regard me as too forgiving. Perhaps I have to be. We might view that as a cause for mitigation in our judgement, but that made very little difference to Bernard, later known as 'Lemongrass.' He was too lost to worry about our judgements.

Perhaps Bernard was never that sure who he was. It was not a question that he seems to have asked with any urgency. In his youth and at college, he had flirted with music at sub-performance levels and thought this interest defined him. In his early twenties, he ignored his limitations enough to work on 'his music' and centred his social life on it. He could be described as a drummer but also played a few well-worn chords on the piano. He could compose songs, and some of his lyrics indicated a melancholic insight, which was more evident as he got older. This fragment of the unique kept his dreams alive until it became clear that no one would pay him to use it.

Again, like many of us, when it came to setting off on the voyage of a working life, his mind was free of definitions, so he pretended to be normal, and had worked since college as a quantity surveyor. Many of us are not defined by our work, or even able to express ourselves through it. We are held in place by a sense of realism and the ability to be a utility in someone else's plan. In this regard Bernard was not unusual.

His vanity – never a dominant characteristic – had been tested early on by baldness, which left the top of his head shining and at the mercy of the sun. At the age of twenty-five, he had married a girl who decided he was reliable, kind, and steady, and for a time, he proved to be a decent provider of an unexceptional home. He had managed this role successfully for fifteen years, but his trips away had gradually prised open the doors of temptation, and he found himself walking through them with some abandon. To start with, it had been what might be called 'professional' ladies, who smiled on demand and might provide other services if you were feeling 'like a gentleman' or simply generous.

Such a course of action would never have occurred to him if someone he was working with and with whom he formed a brief but intense friendship had not suggested that a few doors down the road from the pub where they were drinking, an antidote to the barrenness of life might be available. It was an introduction fuelled by alcohol but, once he tasted this fruit, he was hooked on the flavour.

"Just sit down, darling, and tell me what you like," is much easier on the ear than, "Your report is late," or, "the kids need taking to ballet, and I've a hair appointment."

Over time, his appetites and curiosities grew until his researches on the internet were discovered by his wife, and he was invited to leave followed shortly by his clothes and a number of personal effects, including some magazines discovered in the desk in his 'office,' a room not much larger than a cupboard. That was two years ago. His two daughters had sided with their mother, at least for now, and his life gradually became more isolated, bound by the confines of his lodgings.

Perth, his hometown, is one of the remotest large cities on the planet, but, like all cities, will allow you to slip through the cracks if you become hard to define and unprotected by wealth.

Now Bernard's routine was work – freelancing for an agency – followed by a snack or meals, and films. He disliked violence and fantasies peopled by beings from other planets. He had no patience for sagas filled with ancient gods or vampires or many of the things modern cinema audiences find so captivating. No, he loved romantic comedies and thrillers where semblances of good manners were maintained: films where intimacies might be suggested but not too graphically. He wanted to be reminded of, or even introduced to, a world in which tenderness between people or couples was not a flight of fantasy.

It was a quality which had leeched out of his life. His wife's greatest compliment about him during what might be described as the 'golden years' of his marriage, at least by the unobservant, was that 'he did his duty,' and so it appeared. He just did what people expected because, like me, he had found they would leave you alone, and in appearances, he was an unexceptional, contented family man. I did not meet him until much later, but our closest companions in attitude and habit may be physically thousands of miles away – a truth made more evident by the internet. We were as different as we were similar, Bernard and I, but in passing, you can always recognise another disorientated soul. When we met, we were strangers who understood parts of each other.

In my small world, where everyone's business was shared and commented on, few secrets of any magnitude lasted longer than a week, but in the city, whatever its location, a level of anonymity is not hard to achieve. In fact, it may be difficult to escape from. Later on, I felt a sad kinship with Bernard. We were both loners in different circumstances, and who knows what I would have done in his position? My appetites may not have been the same, but isolation affects us all differently. It is always nice to talk of self-discipline and standards, but as we know from the behaviour of some in public life, they are largely kept in check by lack of opportunity and scrutiny, not by an innate desire to be the perfect man.

Perhaps I am too cynical. Perhaps my own secrecy has robbed me of the ability to visualise the presence of the good in circumstances where controls are minimal.

In watching films, Bernard allowed some light to filter through those unwashed panes of glass he called his eyes and illuminate the softer recesses of his inner being. His secret pleasure was romantic comedies, and he was not selective in his choice of film apart from seldom straying outside this genre. He longed, at least in dreams, to have a moment in which he was a person comfortable with himself, and to be found by a girl who recognised this in him. Some girl, sweet and celebrating, who tended to his wounds and praised him for his qualities. He would never find her and win her for himself. That much truth he owned. But was it possible? Could it happen that some sweet being might rest her gaze on him and see a beauty lost to public gaze?

There, in the darkness of the cinema – his still preferred location – sitting with his popcorn and his coke, he allowed the tightness to grip around his throat and taste his own lament as tears rolled down his cheek. This man, sliding out of youth alone, who had never been kissed by one who thought him precious beyond all things, sought tenderness as if it were the Holy Grail.

He did not read. He only viewed and sometimes dreamt. The taste of longing, however much ignored, became a persistent flavour in his mental diet until, one day, he stumbled on the world of internet dating, where pretty girls smiled out from photographs and asked for fun and the chance to be understood. No research was involved, and money was tight because most went on maintenance and food, but free sites offered some relief and fanned his hopes that all things were still possible.

Initial investigations brought little hope. The girls he liked all seemed so much younger than him, and he lived in fear of ridicule. The quality he found least appealing in the eyes of the opposite sex was knowledge. He wanted a second chance to bathe in innocence and let its sweet, gentle, and forgiving embrace ease his loneliness. But in all this, fear held him in check. How would it be if someone saw his name and sniggered at him as he stood counting bricks? It would be the final humiliation in a life hidden by respectability.

He had a friend, Derek, who had introduced this world to him, casually at first; who, in the absence of other candidates, might be called his closest friend. With him, Bernard went for drinks, and talked about music and the rest. With him, he shared some confidences and laughed and swapped their brand of stupidity. He could voice his opinions as if he were a judge and adopt the manner of a person whose verdict on matters vital should be sought by those 'in the know' if not in power, and Derek did the same. Sometimes they argued, but their friendship was not built on opinions but on appetites: on drink and food and sex, or certainly the lack of it. Thinner, better looking, and with an easier charm, Derek seemed more fortunate with girls than him, but not enough to find some permanency.

Sometimes, as if by magic, Derek's girl of the moment or the week might have a friend who'd ceased to care and fell at the first push. On those sweet nights – brief, if truth be told – they shared the chance to smirk and to pretend that life was good, and they were equals in the pursuit of pleasure.

Apart from sex, they both described themselves as 'foodies' and 'passionate about good music,' whatever that might be. They might be found, bottles in hand and, soothed by a quantity of beer, careless of their age, raising their heads as some guitar solo rose in tortured ecstasy while they relived a sense of freedom enjoyed in some bygone year. But it was through the plate that they would travel the world and grunt their commentary as they weighed up the merits of various cuisines. There was nothing unusual in this activity, which challenged his fragile budget, but the infrequency with which Bernard could 'step out' in anything like style, made it more significant. Of all foods they enjoyed, Thai ranked above the rest.

Throughout their investigations, and whatever the merits of other regions, Thai food always came back to the fore, and it was always a Thai meal that was saved for special occasions: birthdays or the marking of some romance. There was green chicken curry, of course, and then Pad Thai, a timeless favourite, and massaman. The list was not endless, but it was in contemplation of these delicacies that both Bernard and Derek bared their sensitivities. The world of private longings and the ache to leave a life without tenderness Bernard kept to himself and partly from himself. His visits to the cinema and other more intimate venues were not shared. The pleasures of his friendships only extended to weaknesses that where containable. Loneliness, however it was described, was seldom a subject for conversations between males he believed.

~2~

Derek, unlike Bernard, was a naturally cheery 'let's get involved' chappy who liked to be the centre of some attention. Unlike Bernard, he was not squeamish about his effect on others.

"Bernie," he might say, "life is divided between the shitters and the shat upon."

His charm was hard edged, but in the pursuit of what he wanted, he used it to great effect. Many people who he met saw him only once if there was choice, but in his friendship with Bernard, he had found someone tolerant of his strutting and interfering manner. There was no situation anywhere in the world for which he did not have the answer, and he was prepared to offer you his opinion at any length you could handle. He could talk forever about anything, and he never let lack of knowledge come between him and 'the facts' as wished them to be understood. We know the man.

Sometimes, even he realised he was at the outer reaches of his researches, casual at best, and he might add something like, "Let's introduce a working hypothesis," and then proceed to talk nonsense with a confidence and range of language which beguiled those new to his acquaintance. People who were subjected to his windbaggery on a regular basis tended to avoid getting stuck with him for long periods.

The heart of the matter was his appetite for winning. The last word must be his, and all challenges must be bested. It made him hard to like apart from those who gained no sense of his frailties or for whom he held special warmth. So complex was his approach that he would use his frailties to gain him what he wanted, and once this was achieved, hard stare as if to say, "You think I'd show my inner self to you? Don't ring me with your laments."

The danger was he displayed his weakness as a form of bait, but never let you touch it. Those persuaded to move nearer by this guile were used to sate his appetites, and then often left baffled by his sudden change of manner.

Bernard, as we have noted, was an exception to this rule, possibly because Bernard saw beyond the verbal swaggery and a genuine kindness bestowed on a chosen few, or possibly because Derek saw Bernard as ceaselessly gullible and thus amusing to play with. You take your pick. They shared a similar sense of the ridiculous and laughter cemented their affection along with food, music, and their appetite for female company.

Derek advised his friends on all matters from clothes to work and dating techniques. Bernard's wardrobe was a constant source of comment.

"You need to look in a shop window once or twice a year," he'd been known to say, or, "You're going clubbing in that? You look like a gardener," was another classic.

It was understood that Bernard would absorb all such comments with his apparently limitless good humour. Sometimes, their plans met with success. Sometimes, as I've mentioned before, a joint date would lead them both to a successful conclusion and they would sit, metaphorically, on a mountain ridge, admiring the view and savouring their moment of conquest.

It was Derek, of course, who came up with the idea of internet dating after Bernard told him he had been checking out some sites.

"Come on, mate. It's made for you. I'll help you set it up."

On his own, such a thing would never have entered Bernard's head, but his hunger and interest, poorly disguised, made him a wary but then increasingly willing pupil. In the handling of other's lives we are always braver than with our own; so it was with Derek. In some spookily compatible manner, he started shaping Bernard as Katie was developing Misty thousands of miles away.

"It's all in the photo, mate. First things first, we've got to get you some hair."

"Oh, please," said Bernard. "How will I explain that when I see them?"

Derek smiled as one who had conquered both poles and the odd mountain in between. "Let's cross that bridge when we come to it. By then they will be yours, hook, line, and sinker. You'll see. I'll guide you to paradise."

Derek was loving the whole project, and Bernard found himself indulging him. He now approached the idea almost like a game, so they might as well describe him as a giraffe for all the difference it would make.

They toyed with the photographs after a wig was purchased, an event that took up a whole Saturday afternoon, some laughter, and a couple of drinks. Bernard became more and more relaxed and started entering into the adventure. It was like creating a small drama based loosely on his circumstances. Did he seriously think he was going to chat up some lady on the internet and then win her heart over coffee and a range of cakes? It always seemed unlikely, but there was enough temptation in it to drive him forward.

Are there people who survive on impressions? I've always thought so. They create them swiftly, and with some skill, and then move on as if blessed with a non-stick coating before the social auditors have a chance to check on their character. Some of those who met Derek wished he stuck around long enough to have his bluff called, but that seldom happened. The bold hand shake, a brief indication of his career successes put out almost as an aside, his sense of experience – largely gained through the internet – and an ability to dress and groom himself to standards he considered above the average had allowed him entry to places many don't reach and some don't want to. In truth, it was the air of confidence which did it: a strange affectation in the circumstances. His childhood had been marked by signs of chronic anxiety, which might be used by those who had that knowledge to point at inner frailties, but I'm not one for pop psychology. Whatever ghosts lived inside his mind, they appeared to have no impact on his waking hours.

Nowhere was his undoubted skill better exercised than in his dealings with the opposite sex. He had a sister, whom he placed on a pedestal, and whom he treated quite differently to everyone else, but all other women were 'fair game.' Nothing yet had taught him otherwise.

I don't wish to say that he was entirely poisonous, because he was not, but apart from his immediate family and oldest friends, he enjoyed a freedom from concern for others. It was an advantage of sorts.

The world was your oyster, he thought, and if you did not seize it, don't blame others. Bernard was his exception, his protégé, and Derek sought to open his eyes to a world of possibility, if not responsibility.

Bernard's secret tolerance was that he knew all this but somehow didn't mind. He had an acceptance for others' foibles based on the need to live with his own. In contrast to Derek, Bernard was not dishonest with himself, but his quiet sense of moral unease kept him from being too harsh in his judgment of others. His weaknesses, which might stretch out to vices, were a secret from everyone, even the man he regarded as his closest friend. Obviously, through his trawling through porn sites and other avenues of research, he was more familiar with the internet than Derek realised. What he had never considered was internet dating, and Derek was uniquely positioned to help him in this new adventure. He'd used it himself with some success for what he called 'short term hook ups,' which normally meant a weekend or so.

The wig, a no-expense-spared creation in dark brown, did something to make Bernard look a little younger and from a planet nearer home. Normally, his drawn and slightly lined face, together with jug-like ears and baldness, had given him a difficulty with those used to making snap judgements, a characteristic brought into sharper focus on the web and often on dating sites.

Drink and excitement have an effect on judgement, and it was clear that both men were not in full control of their senses.

"Your age," said Derek, "I think we need to shave that a little."

"What do you mean shave?" asked Bernard, not as familiar with bending perceptions as Derek.

"Forty two is a little old in the tooth for our prime market."

"And what is our prime market?" said Bernard, feeling he was drifting further outside his comfort zone. To be fair, he had left it sometime before with the introduction of the wig, but lying about his age was a hard thing to accomplish for a quantity surveyor: one who valued measurement more than understanding.

Of course Derek had the answer. "Look, Bernie," he said — he used to shorten his friend's name when he was being especially cajoling or manipulative — "the world of dating is not one of hard facts."

"But I just want a normal girl. You know. Someone to walk with, watch films with, who can cook and laugh at my jokes."

"What jokes are those Bernie?" replied Derek. "I've never heard you tell one."

Bernard wracked his brain for some gem with which to make his point, but then just shook his head.

"I think we'll go for thirty-two," said Derek. "You could get away with that in the right lighting, and the wig knocks years off you. It opens up the market. Women in their thirties are a bit on the guarded side, and we don't want that do we?" He smiled and flashed his polished teeth at his old chum, who was losing the will to argue. "Let us continue with our creation."

"Alright. Thirty- two."

He would be a surveyor rather than a quantity surveyor. It

never did to be too precise about professional backgrounds.

"Music."

Before Bernard could reply, Derek was already describing his tastes as 'eclectic.' That should give off the vibe of someone who had thought things through and was open to all art forms. More and more, Bernard found himself to be the subject of this profile but not the creator of it. Indeed, the guy with brown hair who was looking at him from the page with a range of vigorous hobbies was so different from himself that he started to abandon all sense of realism.

"Loves skiing, sailing, and the ocean," he suggested.

"You've never been skiing in your life," said Derek, and then they both started laughing.

It was not long before Bernard was a well-read man of thirty-two with a decent experience of life, broad ranging interests, and an appetite for outdoor sports who was looking for a lady of twenty-two to thirty-five to 'join him in life's adventures, both inside and outside the home.'

Bernard thought that suggested an undercurrent of intimacy without being too forward and was likely to attract the eye of any discerning women. Derek was delighted to see the way his protégé was entering into the spirit of their enterprise.

Soon, they were working on a name.

"Stricker," suggested Derek, followed by Sailorman, Music Maker, and A Taste of Life.

After deliberations lasting most of Sunday evening and a further bottle of wine, they came up with. 'Lemongrass,' a possible reference to the green chicken curry takeaway they had both been enjoying. Hippy-esque often attracted those less concerned with hard facts. That was one of Derek's observations, but it had a ring of truth to Bernard, who was now floating gently beyond the borders of realism.

Soon the profile was up and 'live.' Anything was possible now. They set their range of interest at ten miles, and waited for a response, and waited. They both could see that even this new avenue would not get Bernard to paradise over night, but patience was the thing.

"Don't worry," said Derek. "It always takes a couple of days for you to get noticed."

Once he was alone, Bernard played with the settings and looked at a few profiles. Many of them looked very nice and slightly young until he remembered his new age. Just out of curiosity, he changed his setting to two hundred and fifty miles to see what difference it made to his matches. One click showed him that his list of 'likely success stories' based on the quiz he had lied through only a couple of hours before, had changed significantly. This was interesting.

He noticed that whoever he looked at would know he had visited their profile, and he didn't like that, but the simple voyeurism was too tempting for him. It was not until the early hours of the morning that he shut his laptop and retired to bed. For no reason, he felt a breeze move through his life.

"Is it possible?" he thought. Perhaps something could happen. The fabrications paled in his mind beside the urgency of his longing. That he, awkward, shy, and emotionally clumsy now had access to the details of girls he would never know or ever dreamt of talking to in a million years was the miracle of it. He felt something like freedom, and he loved this moment. For the first time in as long as he could remember, he fell asleep with a smile.

Through all these lies, so artfully created with his friend, he touched that sweet innocence, which had lain untended inside his secret thoughts. That dream fed only by the cinema now slept beside him on the pillow and soothed him to delicious sleep.

~3~

Misty was a sweet and gentle creature as far as was known. All of us have an inner and outer life or personality, and usually there is enough harmony between the two to prevent any differences between them causing misunderstandings. Is that too polite a word?

With some people, like Bernard, the urgent voices of his inner life had thrust through the fabric of his public demeanour, and left him exposed and then isolated from his previous personal life and children. Many of us battle with this dialogue to some degree, thankfully less drastically than this.

Misty too, had an inner voice not heard by anyone but herself. She had memories she would not share.

She was a product of her parents. David was his own man, if not aggressively so, and circumstances had allowed him this privilege. His hungers were not personal or intimate. In that way, he knew where he was and trusted Margaret to feel the same. His voyaging was mental and impersonal, looking for patterns and wisdoms not discernible to everyday enquiry, and this search had rendered him slowly more eccentric but still gentle in his curiosity. Margaret had helped to make this possible. They were one of those rare and unusual couples who met at the village school and shared common friends and pre-occupations, who had come together almost as an expression of natural order. Starting out on some grand voyage of discovery was never going to be their thing.

David's father ran a smallholding, and in time, David inherited it and changed its produce to reflect his own interest. As luck would have it, his passion chimed with an appetite for the new and experimental in vegetarian cuisine, and he enjoyed a regular, if not spectacular, income from his land. This suited them both.

Margaret who by nature would have loved a large and sprawling family, suffered from a difficult first birth, and further children became an impossibility. They would not adopt or even consider the idea. Acceptance of what is or what life serves up was at the heart of their behaviour.

They did not travel, had never travelled, and as people do, Margaret filled her heart with her family and the children brought by Misty through her door. Lemonade was offered. I've mentioned that already, but there were cakes and sandwiches. Anything a kitchen could provide as well as warmth and love which leaves all questions at the door. It was an oasis of acceptance but protected by a view of what was right as far as the Potts landscape was concerned. A world where eccentricity was understood, but recklessness was not. Those elements, present in every grouping and locality, which drank from wilder cups than hers, somehow found themselves outside the gate.

Misty was not one to experiment – she shared that with her parents – and her home held no excitement for those seeking adventure fuelled by an appetite for thrills or posturing. Those who strutted their way through youth, and every locality has them, seldom passed her gate and were never invited through it. The only exception to this rule was Katie, whose being and nature were too familiar to be examined, and whose hunger for the new was an echo of some distant relative, or so I always thought.

In families, two sisters can be as different as the hill is from a valley, yet still contain the same minerals. Margaret had walked through youth in slow and certain steps, soon helped on her way by David. Margaret's sister, Sandra, was always the more restless and challenging: the one who sneaked out late at night to party with the wilder boys of the village. She held onto her sanity, but she loved to taste adventure for its own sake as her own mother, Katie's grandmother, now deceased, had described it. In time, she had married Geoff Ballard and succumbed to the benefits of routine, but her dreams, which were more the size of whims, still infected her approach to life. Her daughter was her mother, yet somehow magnified. Her restlessness was more pronounced, even if they shared similar levels of timidity. Through Misty, perhaps, Katie could counter her own lack of nerve. It was not a conscious wish, but her frustrations could make her reckless with her friend.

As Misty grew older, her parents said nothing about their hopes to Misty or each other, but they, too, wished that Misty, just as Margaret had done, might find some steady boy, reliable in his aims who would keep her safely by his side.

Both parents kept their life indoors. Somehow, they were sure, things would be sorted out, and some nice boy would appear in due time. There was no urgency, and Misty seemed happy with her life, although edgier since her college days, just gone. Time, they both felt sure, would settle her back into her normal path. They had little experience of the extraordinary in events or in behaviour and kept worries firmly under wraps. It was their way. Boys showed interest, and Misty's head was full of the dreams a young girl dreams, but somehow no one made that magic leap. A few light dates was all that furnished her young mind with romantic experiences, and even these had been tentative at best.

The warmth of her exterior was all I knew. She had softness, beguiling in its intimacy, but also a sense of privacy which kept boys at arm's length. A soothing antidote to those bleak judgements I received from my own wife, and I had never gained or sought an audience with her heart. As far as was possible, I stayed out of her circle. Although that was hard. Katie was often with her, and our families met as local families do. On occasion, as I have said, she would make her small remarks and indicate that somehow you were a favourite but with no implied invitation. It was un-directed warmth that touched you briefly and then vanished on a breeze. Without trying, she had learnt the secret art of transmitting impersonal affection but always with light feet. Her presence teased me, although her eyes did not. It was the secret of her mystery.

I do not know how 'Lemongrass' first came to her attention, but I do know that somehow he beguiled her. He made her dream beyond the range of facts. He had a small gift in the song-writing sense and wrote lyrics in his time, which gained enough attention to fuel his vanity, possibly above its just deserts or at least back then. In his twenties it had allowed him to dream, but that was long ago. I've told you that as well.

In the evenings, when sitting on his own – not an unusual event – he might sit at his piano, earphones on his head, and sing his songs as if crying a lament. These lyrics written when his spirit was still fluid, reminded him that perhaps he had a life, that not everything was measurement. Who knows the toxic blend when two dreams mix? Can two people, almost by accident, reach across some thousand miles and be the nourishment the other seeks?

Chapter Three

Is there some event, not always publically discussed, by which we measure or sometimes explain our lives? "It would all have been so different if," or, "Without that I might never have managed…" We can all fill in the blanks.

Before she met me, Misty had had such a moment, still hidden from her family. An incident, which might be considered trivial in its way but not to many girls. One you might make light of to yourself, or brave the storm and reveal everything and face a scrutiny few can handle. Misty certainly could not. She had closed the door on candour. Privacy was her sanctuary, protected by her fragile, open manner. Most people were more interested in protecting her than in understanding her. I, sucked in like all the rest, and medieval in my obsessions, began my sweet descent into chaos, motivated by feelings of gallantry, piqued deftly by her expressed frailties. I had no sense that they were manufactured and, I suspect, neither did she. With her, I seem to have no sense at all.

At college, she shared a room with Carol, and they got along pretty well. As luck would have it, Carol was a more immediately open and chatty individual, and through her, Misty met and socialised with a group of people not unlike the girls she knew at home, in character at least. I've said it before: she had a knack of being intimately impersonal. Of putting out selective compliments, but ignoring all the implications.

"Jasmine is so kind, isn't she?" directed at everyone and no one might indicate that they had shared some private bonding, but nothing near that closeness had occurred. It was a nervous habit, an unconscious mannerism possibly made to put people at their ease but also keep their distance. Probing was not welcome. I have no proof of this. Whatever it was, it helped her blend in with her new circle.

Her 'Bill always understands' approach suggested a possibility of warmth, but nothing ever followed the remark. On those brief occasions when we were alone, walking from the pub or maybe at her parent's home, her capacity for suggested intimacy – of somehow indicating that we both knew there was more between us than it was polite to say – was placed on one side. For me, it just hung like a picture in the corner of the room: a tantalising glimpse of a heaven never experienced. I would acknowledge her beauty, but not succumb to it. I always told myself that, but what did I know? Vanity comes in many guises. Mine was in believing myself stronger than I was.

At college she was studious and committed. One of those fortunate people who, from the first sip of milk somehow understood their role in life, at least professionally. She was always going to be an infants' teacher. She loved small children, dogs and cats, and all things which might gather round her chair and not ask probing questions. That is what I believed.

I felt as if I dare not hope, and cannot hope, but cannot not live without it. The fact that I was married seemed to have no impact on my thoughts. My actual position and my imagination had parted company some time ago. I hid all feeling as best as I could, but filled my solitary walks with urgent conversation and debate.

With the outside world, my calmness was my armour, and with David Potts I shared a search for some aesthetic or a definition of the moment, which might encapsulate the entire experience of living. To bury myself in such thoughts, and share them with David was my only disguise, my one chance of escape from making life too personal. When not asleep, I remained always on watch. Some things have not changed. You can see how it was with me. I never got to know what was real or fundamental apart from fear, perhaps. Misty, of whom I'm meant to be speaking, may have been the same. We all have something of that in us don't we? Some questions which will never be answered?

Misty, with Carol and a small circle of girls, formed the habits young girls do, of swapping tales and drinking coffee. Sharing thoughts of home and talks of boys and dreams and sometimes hobbies. None of the people in her group where loud or extrovert, but in each group, leaders will emerge. They have no choice. In Misty's case it was Imogen, a girl from the same year who also lived on the same floor of the hall of residence as Carol and Misty. It was Imogen who normally suggested the agenda, and remaining in the group meant largely falling into her plans. Carol was what you might call 'an alternative voice,' who tagged along as asked but always had a point of view. You might call her the second in command or rival leader with Misty as her acolyte.

All groups are formed by exposure to a common experience, be it college, school, work, or war. The choice is yours but these are the foundations of intimacy for most of us, at least for a time. With the end of school, or college, or whatever, the vast majority of these connections are consigned to memory and wait there till summoned by old photographs. So it was with Misty and her group. They enjoyed a polite and warm companionship but nothing more. They might snigger and laugh and share their stresses of the moment, but not much more than that. They knew 'everything there was to know' about each other, but always at some distance. This was not stated, but between some of them, the search for a deeper bonding could be seen.

By chance, Carol and Misty had that sense of being one layer deeper than the rest. Misty, who looked for guidance in all things, while at college switched her gaze from Katie to her roommate with endearing casualness. Her cultured vulnerability never let her down. Their situation was not unusual. In time, they would drift apart, but back then, they didn't know this. Back then, friendships were forever. We always think that. Many of us are not wise enough to recognise when the best opportunities offer up themselves, and so with Misty, she placed her friendship with Carol on an equal plane with others. Carol, was selfless in her way and protected Misty while others became more engrossed in having fun without regard to cost or consequence. The group was not restless, or bent on wild abandon, but these were college days, away from mum and dad and free at last to walk as they would wish upon a stage built from their own imagination.

Friday or Saturday might find them at a club, dancing in a circle, with handbags all collected in the centre. A conspiracy of politeness rebuffing all enquiries from the boys, at least at first. In time, of course, boyfriends became a fact, and two of them already had beaus, who sometimes travelled up to visit them but otherwise played no part in their routines.

Misty – in my opinion prettier than many – had her fair share of admirers, and always, when the evening was over, the girls lay on their beds back at college and de-briefed the whole experience. It was exciting to be wanted, but also nerve wracking. She had no experience of the personal, apart from with her family, but somehow, she felt differently. Perhaps she was too used to Katie orchestrating her moves to make one on her own. Perhaps her parent's gentle isolation and eccentricities had left her unschooled in lightweight social intercourse. Whatever the reason, she developed the knack of being part of events, but from a distance. In the crowd, but also slightly separate.

In any set of circumstances, there are exceptions, and this one was called Richard.

Richard was a boy with enough sense to bide his time, and who had met them towards the middle of their last year; some post-grad boy with that edge of maturity which marked him out as being civilised; a still young man who had mastered the ability to juggle being 'one of the lads' with discretion of conduct in open society. As such, he was gifted in not setting off any alarms. His ease of manner and unpressured approach made him a safe bet for those seeking companionship without intimacy. This was a manufactured demeanour, as time would tell, but assembled with the highest standards of workmanship. No one I spoke to later was aware of any shadows in his manner.

In Carol's view, he was a more than suitable date for Misty in contrast to those other boys whose agendas were quite predictable. With Richard, coffees were followed by meals and sometimes walks, and gradually, Misty felt her guard relax. There was no passion, but an easy companionship, which never challenged her privacy.

A visit to the cinema seemed free of risk, and found them sitting somewhere near the back in a near empty studio to watch a film, somewhat obscure, which satisfied a new fashion for researching 'world cinema.' It would be something to talk of with her dad, and convince him that she was more than cotton wool. The film played out, with a distinguished slowness of plot, which they followed through subtitles. The film was Portuguese or Brazilian, she was not sure, but it was gentle and observant. She liked that.

They munched their popcorn and drank from a shared carton of drink – an intimacy which no longer seemed forced. He made no move to suggest it applied any licence. The film moved on and absorbed them both, or so it seemed. Somewhere towards the end, his arm moved round her, and she stiffened slightly, but nothing else was tried, and gradually she relaxed. A semblance of intimacy was to be expected at this stage, and she had no wish to be thought cold, so she snuggled slightly to demonstrate her acceptance of the move.

Suddenly, and without commentary, the screen blanked out, and his face moved over hers. His tongue was forceful, and his hand moved up under her shirt and across her breast. The whole thing was so fast, she had no time to think. Then she tried to squeal, but his mouth still covered hers. His grip grew tighter, and she could hear his breathing grow more ragged through his nose. He seemed to have become some kind of animal, a stranger full of appetite and now controlled by lust. The civilised boy was gone, and this crude being destroyed her privacy. His hands became swiftly more aggressive, invading her without feeling. Wriggling was no use as he lifted up her bra and tugged and pulled at her reluctant flesh. There was no diplomacy. Her skills were gone or useless, cast aside. Panic was her only emotion. That and fear.

At last, she managed to escape and, without speaking, rushed out of the stalls and to the streets now shrouded in dusk where the lights covered everything with their orange glow. Her tears were blurring out her vision, and her feet just walked to 'get away from here,' from violation and distress.

How could this happen? How had she been so stupid? She walked and walked and walked and finally found herself in some café late at night, drinking coffee, and staring out of the window. The owner, some elderly gentleman not used to seeing young ladies on their own at this late hour, paused to enquire if she was alright, but something in her manner said 'do not disturb' so he did not, but watched her nonetheless. Gradually, she calmed down enough to return to her hall of residence, and, as dawn approached, re-entered her room and quietly got undressed. Conversation was the last thing she required. She felt as though some familiar hamper in her world had opened up and poisonous snakes had slithered into her life.

Luck was with her in that finals were near at hand and weekend partying was not much enjoyed. Richard made no move to call, and when Carol asked where he had gone Misty just said, "It didn't quite work out." In truth, she'd had enough. She just wanted to go home.

Why it is that these apparently shameful events are sometimes hidden by the victims is hard to understand, and yet not hard. The sense of feeling a fool, exposed, laid bare, of wanting to bury the whole episode behind her practised smile and make believe that such urgent primitive moments were not part of her life. All these were there, but most of all, as she lay in her bed, night after night, the sense of violation would not leave. Those grubby hands pawing at her flesh, she felt them every day.

Her behaviour changed, but not too obviously. The general manner was the same, but somehow more guarded. No more dates were sought or suggested. Carol suspected something might have gone wrong, but waited for her friend to tell her how. Misty never did, but in her eyes – once open to fresh light – a guarded edge marred her previously innocent expression. At home, she received the same caring and unconditional love as always, but there is another side to 'caring unconditional love.' Sometimes, those who have nurtured you from a young age, and provided the shape and environment of your childhood can feel partly that they own you, or at least demand you exist without changing, that you always will remain their sweet, their darling, the precious child or sibling. To demand the right to change or act outside the accustomed shape always presents problems. That is how it seems to me.

Although outwardly unchanged, Misty was aware of a new and guarded side to herself, and that her parents were unsettled by it. Her innocence now seemed forced, even to herself. They, who believed always that nothing happened which might not be known or discussed were regarded as too un-worldly to share her experience. In the past, she had been too innocent as well. An incident of little importance to some, for Misty became a defining moment of her youth: the embodiment of fear and its power to mark your life.

~2~

On Friday afternoons, Bernard sometimes found himself without appointments, and this is when he visited his secret world. Often, he would seek out some new romantic comedy and allow himself to wallow in his dreams. About once a month, he paid a visit to Ruby, which may or may not have been her real name. There were intimacies, of course, and that brief moment of juddering oblivion when all thoughts vanished into pleasure, but mainly it was to lie with her on the bed and just talk and hear her ask him for advice as though he was a real and special man.

She had the knack of greeting him with an air of relief when he came through her door, as if he was a cut above the rest. Someone uniquely connected to her, and with whom she shared a bond more precious than all others, some beautiful conspiracy full of unspoken promise. In her company, enjoyed without judgement, he became more confident and would tell stories, acting out the characters and sometimes putting on accents to make the whole thing seem more real.

"Oh, Bernard," she said, "you make me laugh so. You should have been on the stage."

And yes, he should have, he now thought. Only in her company was that strutting persona allowed the space to walk, as she, delighted, admired his each and every turn and posture.

Lying there unclothed, and letting his eyes drift across her naked body, he treated her with gentle respect. This vessel of sweet womanhood, who offered him acceptance without him having to justify himself. He might lie on his back, while she lay beside him, leaning on her elbow, as he shared some dull event from his week, and she would laugh or smile touched with just the right degree of naturalness to make him feel that, somehow, this was real. This precious time. This simple time with a being for whom no pretence was necessary and who would not judge him.

They had their little rituals. For this sweet hour or maybe a bit more, she was no clock watcher, especially for her regulars, and part of it was her joining him in the shower.

"Your back is really nice you know," she might let slip, or, "You have such gentle eyes."

Compliments general in themselves, but also real enough to make him think that here, within this fragile rented hour, he'd found a women who finally understood the heart of what it was that made him breathe.

He was not stupid, or not in many things, and rationally, he pretended all was false or not serious or 'up for grabs,' but somewhere in his heart, she touched the lock which kept his naked longings from the street. That was her skill, which no one could replace. How else would she touch him as she did? In outlook or position she seemed almost like him, an outsider hanging on to life and distrusted in most company, who could never say what she did or felt. Well, nor could he. That was their bond. Their secret complicity.

Afterwards, sated but uneasy, he adjusted to life in public scrutiny and wondered, as he drove his car, if that had been quite real. Oh, how he wished, perhaps, that he could turn around and knock on her door and not find Stan or Wayne or some other male cluttering up the borders of his fantasy. How she would welcome him back inside and say, "You felt it too," and fold herself against his chest. Just another body lost in life, who in his presence, felt herself whole again. He dreamt that all the time, but never with such urgency as when he was driving back to his home and wondering if some faint trace of her sweet perfume might still linger on his clothes.

Once inside, he put the kettle on, made himself a coffee, and looked out of the window, staring at the park beyond. His rooms were in the attic of the house, and the view was one of its small perks. Often, in the grip of his rare and tender emotions, he might sit down at his small electric piano and regurgitate one of those songs he penned in the days when he thought his sensitivity might be recognised and expressing it might become his future.

He sat down and let his fingers move over the familiar chords until the trusted melody woke his memories from their slumber and he began to sing his own lyrics.

"Love's outside;

I thought I saw him in the street.

I thought he smiled as I passed.

Not quite there,

Not quite clear, beyond my call."

His voice, although slightly thin and with limited register, was still surprisingly tuneful and had gathered compliments in his past. He let the piano play again, improvising more richly as the mood overtook the sombre realities of his daily life and left him edgily aware of the beauty and impermanence which affects us all. Again he sang, another verse:

"Love's outside;

He never seems to make a fuss.

Full of life, but not for us.

Not for me,

Not this time, beyond my call."

The music was his anthem, and the words a definition of his

outlook as an exile from tenderness. How he longed to love and feel that soft awareness touch his cheek. At last, he stopped and looked up at the clock. In half an hour, he would be meeting Derek for his Friday night drink, and he must be another man then. He changed his shirt, somewhat reluctantly, because Derek, who could be sharp when it was least wanted, was both his closest friend and the last person he would bare his soul to on such matters.

That he might sit at this piano while Derek listened and sing that soft lament he had just sung was never going to happen. Those days of private delusion were gone. Such a moment would invite him to ridicule. He wanted to be loved, certainly, but he had no wish to destroy himself.

Like all men pretending to be tough manly men, they would meet for a drink, but often, as tonight, somewhat curiously, they would go back to Bernard's flat, because it had a bigger kitchen and actually try and cook those dishes they loved so much.

It was a new and exciting expression of their friendship, prompted by Derek recently remarking at some restaurant that, "He could cook much better than this garbage." A slightly crude and possibly harsh verdict on the meal before them.

Neither of them analysed the activity, and there was a discrete understanding that this might be a trifle girlie, but who was to know, and who could say. Perhaps one day, they might open a restaurant together and find themselves the talk of Perth.

"Excellence is our starting position," said Derek with a solemn delivery, which might indicate to the casual listener, that he had just said something profound. In truth, the saying was for display purposes only and carried little truth in it. In time, it might become a joke between them. Perhaps their golden period was still ahead.

Derek already felt himself to be in his prime, but he was always ready to discuss a new venture. With him, the first simple, but quality restaurant would soon become a group and then a chain and finally an international byword in quality dining. How this was to happen, he never specified, but his ability to draw out dreams to their most extreme conclusion, and at the speed of light, in a manner which suggested that it was just a matter of time, but not of doubt, made him powerfully beguiling with those new to his company.

Only Bernard, who had heard of many such schemes, was willing to ignore experience and his own scepticism and enter fully into the excitement. It was part of the bond which protected them from the ordinary dimensions of their lives.

~3~

How would I view all this? This stuff with Bernard and the girl, Ruby? Horror and fascination, I suppose. Let me explain, to myself and you.

All my life, I wanted to be normal, as we all do, but normal is not anybody, but just what everybody thinks it is. I was raised a Catholic boy, educated at a Catholic school. Just like all the other Catholic boys I went to mass each Sunday, ate fish on Friday, and went to confession regularly to admit a range of sins to some stranger, which did not get near to describing the infamy that was in their hearts. I stole a pen, but did I say so? No, because the priest was also a teacher, and who knows what he would have done? From the age of fourteen, I had a crush on Miss Heslop, the art teacher, who seemed a bit freer and less formal than anyone else. My thoughts on her were carnal, and I was always trying to catch glimpses of her body. Did I say that? No. The priest was also my teacher and you know the rest.

My father was a man of austerity and social observance. He believed in fulfilling the expectations placed on him by his profession and social position. His attitude to his faith was never disclosed. He was careful not to utter random and inconsequential opinions. All he required was that I would do as he would wish, and observe the requirements of his published faith. As a lawyer and senior partner of a successful law firm he made few statements which could not be cross-referenced and validated. Passion was not for public consumption. I never saw him lose his temper. He had no interest in my beliefs as such.

That was a personal matter and thus of little interest.

I had moments of intimacy with Katie but not frequently. She was not a girl to mess her hair or makeup in the search for release, and that took a burden from my shoulders. Our relationship, like many relationships, even at the beginning, was built on trust and mutual need, but was largely free of confessions or shared fantasies. Increasingly, on my part, this was cemented by my acceptance from her family. They truly had become my first and only family, and nothing was more important to me than their respect. David Potts, her dad, the fishmonger…

I could go on, but won't.

Collectively, they gave me a sense of belonging, of being accepted and considered part of a circle that nothing else in my life had provided. It was a prize won by accident but now valued beyond measurement.

There was a warmth to Katie, in that she trusted me to be both loyal and boring, and in her way she offered the same to me. She could be capricious and wilful but never to the point of self-destruction. There was an unspoken understanding that she could act as she wanted because I was as I was. Although with limitations, and marred by my secrecies, the relationship had a deep affection, which made the whole performance bearable. My forbearance of her manner was part of the secret of my acceptance. With her parents, with David and Margaret and others in the village, I had earned the right to membership by taking care of one of their own. That is what I believed and I played the role for all that it was worth.

In my search for 'normalcy' I now viewed physical urges as threatening chaos. Thus to live as Bernard did, and allow his central definition, as I saw it, to leak away in whimsical fantasies about this girl he paid to kiss him was hard for me to understand. In our isolations and the fruitless search for balance, we seemed as two souls on the same quest, but our methods and our 'sense of being' separated us. You could not fool me with a smile. That was my boast. With Misty, I sometimes felt a drunken wish to share myself, but still, I remembered her speech with me was her speech with everyone. She had not singled me out. She merely spoke as if she did, and I still knew that.

Bernard paid women to kiss him and somehow thought, behind the hard cash and practised smile, a real affection lay. Who was he fooling? I cannot say, and yet whatever the different routes we had taken, we both seemed to have arrived at a place of personal isolation and tragedy, and neither of us knew how to escape from it. How different was I from this odd misguided man in a wig, with false hobbies, and a secret vice? Not as much as I would like. Perhaps not different at all.

The same truth, I reflected, can be expressed through many different metaphors. He wanted to lose himself in flesh or intimacy, and I wanted to protect myself from these two illusions by means of thought and definition. I know why I adopted mine, but what made Bernard follow his, I cannot say. Both strategies now seem hopeless, but it's easy to say that in hindsight.

I had physical urges. I was not entirely celibate, but I admired the monks who were. Not necessarily in the way of faith, because I did not really have that. Few who witnessed the antics of the priests could leave school without having their beliefs challenged. No, what I envied was the definition behind their isolation, their lack of need for comfort in their search for the absolute. That's what I understood and admired and the quest I had often returned to after a period of chaos.

Bernard's search for salvation relied too much on the whims of others: of mingling two dreams to create a single flawless whole. I had no wish, as far was possible, to serve defenceless as a player in the unfolding of another's drama.

~4~

Sometime late at night, when the cooking triumph had been prepared and eaten, Bernard found himself once more on his own. The strange thing was – or not that strange given Derek's ways – was that the new dating venture had not been discussed.

In many ways this, was a relief. But still…

Now here Bernard sat, late at night, and not entirely sober, looking at the matches on his list. Some people had already viewed him, and this was exciting. Not all was lost. He smiled despite himself and even left a message on some profiles. Nothing much, but just to say thanks for passing by.

"What questions can I answer?" You never know. That might just pique their interest. The fact that the man looking at him from his profile was almost unrecognisable no longer seemed to matter. He knew who he was. Nothing else touched him at this hour.

He clicked around the site, learning the navigation, and entering terms which might change his selected matches. At last, almost on a whim, he changed the distance he would seek his dream. The last choice was 'anywhere' and that was good enough for him. Job done, he turned away to rest.

His time with Derek, Ruby, and this site. It made the world seem slightly fresher, more open, more… He could not find the word, but who cares? Sleep found him contented in his hesitant way.

Chapter Four

My father was a man of definitions, not intimacies. Most famous among his circle was his 'time to taste ratio,' in which the quality of a meal was principally defined as being dependant on the amount of time taken in its preparation. Wasting time was a cardinal sin. Spending hours producing something mediocre went unremarked. This approach typified his attitude to all things. My homework, time allocated to play, room tidiness. The list was pretty endless. My mother, possibly from exhaustion, had died when I was ten and not been replaced. He may have had 'friends' but that was not discussed or disclosed to me.

At ten, I was, in his opinion, old enough to take responsibility. If I strayed he might say something like, "The age of reason is seven William; seven, not eight or nine or ten. Kindly reflect on consequences before acting rashly. Your pocket money is halved this week."

He was the self-made son of a father who had struggled all his life and died before I was born. I'm only guessing, but I suspect the idea that I might somehow take after my grandfather filled him with undisclosed horror. I know his own childhood had been filled with constant moving, visits from bailiffs, and an unremitting air of crisis.

Somehow, by force of will, he had done well at school and university, and at the time of his death – which was recent as you shall hear – he headed a sizable legal practice in the city. It suited him. Making judgements, allocating blame was his preferred approach to life, at least as seen from his son's perspective. He brought the system home. Another of those pithy axioms with which he marked my childhood was, "Remember, if you have a problem, no one else is interested. Solve it yourself."

He belonged to a club, of sorts. For networking purposes, I presume, and playing cards. I was never invited. I have never been there, so I can hardly speculate about its interior or the culture within its walls, but I fear it took boring as an attribute. I might be wrong. Needless to say, I grew up quite isolated and used to my own company. I longed to impress him and aped his lack of emotion and detachment. I still do.

In his sixties, he still worked all the hours without the financial need to do so. He had no hobbies of any depth. For holidays, he would send me off to play with his sister for two weeks in the summer – quite a different sort of life – and I would play with my young cousins, all of whom lived in cheerful chaos quite different from my home. Holidays or hobbies, in his opinion, smacked of a lack of concentration. I am not saying he never took any holidays, but they were brief, modest, and uneventful. There are no photographs.

He was punctilious about the rituals of his religion, but he made no verbal comment on it. I always suspected it was a social matter more than a question of faith. Speculation about what he considered as subjective areas of life were not a thing to waste your time on. I do remember him describing Handel's *Water Music* as 'nice,' but that was about as wild a remark about something which could not be measured, weighed, or hanged as I ever heard him make. He was a fan of the death penalty on the grounds of cost and efficiency. I suppose it went with his legal work. Again, it was as near passionate as I remember him being.

My father was always my idol, not my friend. Somehow, I don't know why, I ended up calling him 'Father' rather than 'Dad.' It says it all really, and might explain why I am as I am. Those softening female influences had no place in his ordered routine. My school was boys only, so it occurred that women were a source of interest, but not familiarity. Only my aunt, podgy, jolly, and unrelated in her manner to her brother, allowed me any access to the mysteries of the female mind. Otherwise, I was unschooled in matters female.

Do you see how I phrase that? That is my father speaking. As I grow older, I discover his unconscious presence in my actions. His shadow is somehow always at my side, commenting on my sad lack of direction or ambition.

"Be careful how you make your bed, William. Expect no help from me." This sentence or others like it were spoken by him to me on more than one occasion.

At the age of twenty-two, I left an ordinary university with an upper, second-class degree in Art History ("Is that really a university subject these days," my father said) and been welcomed with a meal out to celebrate my 'triumph.'

At the end of it, he said in a voice showing few traces of emotion, "As I'm sure you realise, your childhood is now over, William. I expect you to be looking for lodgings and be out of the house by the end of the month. Needless to say, you are always welcome to visit on holidays, birthdays, and Christmas, of course. At Christmas an over-night stay would certainly be in order." Detached as his pronouncement was, it was not shocking if you knew the man. I was not surprised as such, but felt uneasy about making my own way.

At least I had my aunt, who lived outside Birmingham, and whose husband had introduced me to the soothing qualities of beer. How two families could be so closely related and yet be so different in culture and outlook was a mystery I never got near solving. On reflection, the difference between Katie's mother and Mrs. Potts was almost as marked. It may be a thing in families. I agree that if my mother had lived for longer, my childhood might well have been very different. My father was not one for looking back or expressing regrets, so it is hard to say how he felt about the matter.

With Katie, who was always very socially conscious and whose pride seemed to dominate much of her interactions, anything which blemished her profile was a source of embarrassment and shame. It was at least four years after we were married that she revealed her mother had had an affair while she was still young and newly married with someone she met from a town some miles away. I don't know how. Who cares? I didn't, but apparently Katie did. How or why her mother had found herself in this position, I do not know, and I would not ask her, but I admit the idea of her enjoying some reckless 'after hours' fun is hard to reconcile with her current primness and all round social conservatism. Whatever the history, Katie was aware of it. It was a blemish on the costume of a women who valued appearances highly. Once she told me, I never mentioned it again. What would have been gained? But you should have seen the awkwardness with which she told me. She was not sober at the time.

She was as different to me as you could imagine, but we shared several attitudes. Neither of us were that emotionally outgoing. We like predictability, and I was a man of entrenched routine, no doubt inherited from my father, which gave her something to rail against. Nothing there to build a marriage on, perhaps, but who knows what the requirements are. Certainly not me.

Like my father, I saw myself as a man of definitions and not of intimacies, and to be trite, Katie seemed to be more a woman of impulse than planning. What had drawn me to her was her enthusiasm and excitability. They say opposites attract, and that is all I'm left with. Was it a case of mistaken identities? So many relationships are. Perhaps my ordinariness helped me fit in with her family and gave her a profile of wanting the 'right things.' I'm stumbling round for explanations, but I have no real conclusions.

For all I know, this being 'Mr. Conventional' was a big part of my attraction. That Katie, who had presented her parents with so many 'wronguns' could arrive at last with someone so apparently conventional may have surprised them. It's only a theory. Time and boredom have led to changes in her manner.

"Have you ever taken a risk?" she asked me once.

Of course, I longed to say, "Only in marrying you," but I kept my silence, as I had to. In truth, there was far more to my history before meeting her than she could guess at. In my youth,

I had been more destructive and wayward than my current circle would ever imagine. It might be the case that, in some way, my true nature was now in hiding, and I always dreaded its reappearance.

Without realising it, Misty kept tempting it to reappear.

The growing distance between us meant further removal from her family and Misty. Such a thing was more than I could bear. Katie was often contemptuous in her manner and frustrated by my lack of 'show.' My wardrobe was modest, despite her best endeavours, and practical while hers had a certain style, I admit, but also little regard to cost. I pretended to regard her extravagancies with amusement, both with her and in company, yet they always unsettled me. Up to the events I am describing, it is fair to say, no special pressure, apart from her boredom had been exerted on our relationship. We took the situation as read. Possibly it was, in hindsight, an accident waiting to happen.

~2~

I'm not sure when the dating saga started, but I think I know why.

Katie was always trying to 'sort out' Misty with one of the local boys and was gently deflected because they were too short, tall, fat, smoked, or any other failing which came to mind. What was never disclosed was Misty's episode at college with Richard. No one knew of that. The upshot was Katie turned to internet dating.

It was a fresh challenge, a new enthusiasm, and Katie loved those. Making the profile, fussing over pictures, and dictating what they required in a man... What could be more fun than that? Like eating at some restaurant built in paradise. Because they were not lying – after all, Misty was twenty-two and above averagely pretty – making the profile did not take as long as some, at least at first. Saying what she was seemed easy. Saying what she wanted was harder because, as always, they were saying what Katie wanted: quite a different thing. By the time Katie had finished their sporty, outward-bound hero with a poetical soul and an eye for fine cuisine might be easily available, but was not exactly what Misty really wanted.

You know longing. I do. It's with me every day, but those with plenty have something else which must be recognised: the need for peace and the space to make their own choices. Misty wanted that. Already, she had been assaulted by a man who could have entered any living room in any society and been called a 'gentleman.' Now her attitude was very different and guarded, even if her wariness was shielded from most observers, and Katie often got irritated that Misty seemed so hard to please.

Who knows what secrets lay behind a manner or neat appearance? Every soul had a snake within it, Misty feared, and gaining her trust might be like opening a lock without a key: a near impassable barrier.

It was Katie, to be fair, who set the search area at 'anywhere.' She wanted to see what was 'out there' and scanning the world seemed as good a start as any. There is a natural voyeur or window shopper in all of us. We all like to speculate without responsibility. Katie was not alone in that, and Misty was much happier in the general than the particular.

Left to her devices, Misty scanned the site again and tweaked her profile as if toying with her food. 'Sensitive' and 'tender' were two terms she entered into the characteristics she sought. The magic was that each change she included made a subtle difference to her list of favoured matches until at last, by chance or fate, her eye settled on 'Lemongrass.' Possibly it was the name. Not your usual choice, but there was also something gentle in his look which attracted her. More than anything, she discovered, she wanted someone who needed her and would not strut to prove it. She hated show-offs and easy-banter types. In Lemongrass, she sensed an awkwardness and diffidence of manner. How she could pick that up, I do not know, but perhaps it was in a later adjustment made by Bernard after Derek had lost all interest in the adventure.

Bernard had included a little poem, written by himself, which spoke of his non-specific longing for a tender connection, an undisclosed shyness.

"Perhaps in the corner of your soul,
Lives a memory intact, of some life past,
Where we stood on shores yet undefined,
And stared towards a common future".

I'm not saying it was the greatest verse ever written, but there was something in it for Misty.

"Lives a memory intact, of some life past."

Oh, yes, how special that would be. She had always had dreams of reincarnation. She dreamed, sometimes, that this would not be our only life experience, and that we were on some great journey or quest which we shared with 'soul-mates' who we searched for in every life.

How romantic it would be if this was him, so far away but somehow calling out to her. She looked at everything, and not all of it was perfect. That sporty bit was nowhere near her taste, but those sweet lines kept speaking to her till finally she left a little message in his box.

"I love your poetry. Did you write it?"

What harm was there in just asking a simple question. The man lived as far away as you could get, but that somehow made it all the more romantic. It felt like being marooned on some island far from land and seeing a tiny beam of light and sense of life. Would he see her torch waving in the distance and bother to respond?

Had he been nearer, she never would have bothered, but at this distance she could afford to dream without attracting danger. Some man so far away, what could he do? And yet she felt connected all the same.

She checked the time difference on the internet and found out that he was almost certainly asleep. It was six in the evening here so there it would be two in the morning, and he must be dreaming. She closed her laptop and went out to seek her mum. She's done enough probing for the day, but still she felt a soft new light chase shadows from her life.

"How stupid of me," she thought and tried to put the matter from her mind.

Later, she told me that she didn't know why, but initially she kept the connection from Katie. She didn't want Katie 'taking over.' That's what she said.

"She was always so controlling, and I just wanted to have the moment to myself."

It was one of those statements which drew us closer. I knew just what she meant. Secrecy is often the strategy of the socially awkward or shy. I knew that to my cost, and we were both minions of Katie's imagination and used to being tossed around by her whims and vagaries. To be fair to Katie, Misty was a more willing victim than I, and less practised at those techniques of polite deviousness which I used to protect my inner space. Normally, Misty was happy to have her agenda arranged for her. It was what had always happened, but just this once, and for reasons which were not clear, she kept this little moment to herself.

As chance would have it, Katie and I were over at the Potts' that evening, together with Katie's mum and dad and a few other select folk from the village. I'm not sure how it started, and it seemed rather out of character to me, but David Potts had an annual event around his crop of sweet corn. He picked a sizable crop and boiled it there on his farm out in the open and washed down with mugs of home-made cider. It was a jolly event, and I would bury myself in the cooking or cleaning the outside leaves from the corn or some other silent task and hide my interests as far as I could do.

I watched Katie, always in her element where there was noise, and even David Potts giving in to laughter and Margaret fussing over sandwiches and drinks, and other guests asking general questions. It was a village episode. As always, behind my quiet civility and crafted open manner, I kept my eye on the company and especially on Misty who looked so pretty in that yellow dress. Diaphanous and floaty and moving easily as she walked. In these circumstances, at events deeply entrenched in her calendar and with people she knew as well as she did herself, her manner was more open, and for me, infinitely captivating.

She seemed flirty in an innocent way. She and Katie stuck together, moving through the group.

"Two peas," said Stan the ironmonger, nodding his head in their direction, and his comment brought out a smile in those around him.

Katie and Misty, their friendship was a force of nature. Everyone remembered Katie as a young girl, pushing the pram holding her baby cousin, or later, walking her to school. Both junior and senior schools where in the same building in this small village.

I could go on of course but significantly, on this special day marked by familiar celebrations, Misty's mind and heart were already on a journey of some distance, as the man who piqued her interest lay sleeping and unaware of the changes he had started.

~3~

I was a monk, of course. The worshiper of the selfless act. The man who rose above it all and saw the beautiful in the absolute. I told myself that all the time, and in truth I really wanted to be that man. I was that man. Whenever I managed to do some passing kindness without agenda, I felt something like release, as though I'd found my purpose, my station, or my calling, but there was another side to me, too dangerous to consider. I had an unhealthy longing for connection or emotional intensity, it was not a new affliction.

Before Katie, my constant search for this connection, for a blend of reckless passion with integrity, a mix not recorded in civilised history, had got me into trouble more than once: a longing which threatened to unmask me as a man of clay and not the slightly old-fashioned individual of obsessive routine and slightly dated manners I wished to be. With Katie and her family and the solid unquestioning rituals they lived by, I felt I had found the final antidote to this destructive recklessness, but now it was reappearing once again. How much I wanted to put all that behind me, but Misty, with disturbing innocence, kept asking my demons out to play.

A couple of months before the corn party, I had been up in the local big town doing some work for a company and found myself at leisure for a period in the morning. I got myself a paper and went to a café in the square for a coffee. The paper was full of its normal nonsense and title-tattle, but for some reason, I could not sit easily on my own without a book or paper, so always had or brought one. It didn't mean I had to study them too closely, but it gave me a reason to be there and made me feel less exposed to scrutiny.

What I often did when away from my own town, and did that day, was let my eye wander, and pass over young waitresses and allow my secret hungers room to breathe. I was always guarded with my glances, but still, it fed my appetites for fantasies I kept strictly to myself.

On this day, some girl with a foreign accent and shiny black hair, with a slightly arrogant, strutty walk who had caught my eye bent down at the table opposite mine to wipe the surface with a cloth. My eyes moved furtively to her cleavage, now more on show than normal, till suddenly, with that sixth sense that women have, she felt my gaze and raised her eyes to mine. She said nothing, but her look held a rebuke mixed with disgust. I had violated her in some way, and I was full of shame and rather more embarrassment. My action was so far outside my published manner that I would have died if this act became known. I was happier to be considered as a man without hormones than as a pervert. I was not that, I felt sure or hoped, but my longings had made me unmannered.

I hated this behaviour in myself. It had not always been there. Somehow, over the course of my married life, despite my warm relations with her kin, the role of being a shadow in my wife's routine had left me desperate for some display of warmth. I felt myself fantasising all the time, and yet I was aware how unhealthy this was. How distasteful it was. I was not a man given to self-loathing and largely regarded myself as a benefit to those who knew me, but this… This secretive and unsettling behaviour threatened to expose me to shame and ridicule if I was not careful. Now in known company I watched my eyes, but it almost seemed a muscular struggle of will.

What kind of man was I becoming? Hard as it was, I kept my eyes firmly on neutral objects. I found this small act of concentration exhausting.

Chapter Five

You know that feeling when you throw a ball high into the air and see it pause at the summit of its trajectory? I call that the 'weightless moment,' that brief period where gravity is suspended, and we might imagine a glimpse of another life, free of tensions and with different possibilities. I had that now, at the corn party.

Everything seemed sharper and thrown into relief. There was David in his unusual social mode and Margaret ministering to everyone as she always did. Their friends and villagers enjoying the customs of the feast and letting go of their anxieties. At the heart of it was, for David at least, the sense that, somehow, his Misty had come home. She seemed lighter on her feet, and more relaxed in company. His friends noticed it, too. It was one of those rare occasions when everything falls right, and we can just enjoy being friends without a sense of change or outside threat.

This is what I loved. This delicious intimacy, so far removed from my own youth. Of people laughing at familiar jokes, and tolerating each other's eccentricities. Very possibly I over-emphasised the intimacy but I believe that was forgivable.

During this party, I just did my bit: fetching glasses, helping with the corn and, to be fair, both Misty and Katie helped as well. Even Katie's mum seemed more relaxed and leant a hand, pouring drinks and generally pitching in. Katie's dad, of course, was always on hand. I could go on. It was a hands-on, family affair with little formality.

The butcher, not to be outdone, always brought a pig to roast and settling the pig on the spit was part of the tradition and excitement. As for the corn, the locals turned to sages, or foodies if you will, and discussed the flavour, comparing it with the previous year.

"Not a bad one, Davie. I think you've got it right," and, "You can't beat freshness. That flavour is beyond delicious," spoken like an authority.

"Oh you would know," said Nigel, "as you live on bread and beans," and people laughed as people do when they see friends teased without malice and included in the warmth.

Like everyone else, I had no clear reason for the change, but in this brief and sainted hour, I just let myself float away on my sense of community. Drink in hand, and fed and entertained, I looked around at my new family and smiled. Not mine, of course, but now they felt that way, these people who had made their hearth my home. The sentiments welled up inside me, and in the midst of this small paradise, stood Misty, slim and small and smiling, full of tenderness, or so it seemed to me. Her eyes so blue, shining with a non-specific joy. There was a snake in this paradise, and I knew it was residing in my own heart. Hiding within me was the unspoken love, which if given voice would caste me into a wilderness of my own making. I would never risk such exile.

There was another side to Misty, which perhaps I have not explained. Yes, she was more than averagely pretty and with an unspoiled manner, which is rarer than we'd like, but there was this other aspect. Even before going away to college, as a young girl first aware of boys, she had a bit of a reputation as an ice maiden. Certainly, to have had her on your arm would have been a prize indeed, but already she had learnt the skill of being warmly elusive, almost like an air hostess who will do anything you want as long as you don't want it.

To put it crudely, there were easier targets. Girls who were not the sole owner of their parent's love, who lived in a more connected way, far from wind turbines and a fascination with essences. It was not that she was snobby or superior, far from it, but the ordinary and everyday did not appeal to her as it did most girls. That is one of the things which made her friendship with Katie so surprising, but then she'd been in thrall to Katie forever and patterns are hard to break.

One thing which was a bit unusual about this feast was the presence of some young lad who was serving as the apprentice to a builder refurbishing the Hall. As always in these close communities, temporary visitors were also granted temporary citizenship, and during their stay, were included in all events. This young lad, a cheeky, cheery soul with open face and rough cut brown-blond hair, didn't pause to sniff the wind or size up the country or indulge in any subtlety. Oh, no, he just waded in.

He walked up to Misty in his cheery way and said, "Hello, darling, fancy going for a walk?"

"That's very kind," she said. "I've got to help my father."

"Not now, silly," he replied, his grin all wide and friendly. "'Ow's about tomorrow, if it ain't raining."

"I think I'm busy then," she said and moved to turn away.

But he just said, "Well then I'll keep on asking, and you'll join me in the end."

His boss caught his eye, and warned him not to push his luck, and that was fair enough, but still, it was another pause for thought. Misty, who had deflected almost any type of advance, was not so used to this open friendly manner. It didn't disconcert her as such, but it made her think. People around smiled as if the exchange was on a television show. They knew he stood no chance, and the charm was in his innocence.

Katie, of course, had a point of view.

"What have you got to lose? If you're worried, I can keep you company."

"I'll wait and see," said Misty, "I've a few things on my mind."

"What things?" demanded Katie.

But was just told, "This and that."

Katie knew enough not to push her luck, but that meant nothing. She'd just keep on until she'd ground Misty down. The technique had always worked. New faces were always interesting to Katie, even those ones who lacked a little 'class,' not that she would ever consider herself a snob. Was she a snob? Well I would not hold my breath on that one.

The cause of Misty's hesitation, apart from limited interest, was now fast asleep on another continent. Already, he was fuelling her sense of independence. She might be opening the door on a new life, but that was still her secret.

The redeeming feature of Katie's wilfulness was that she, herself, often lost interest in a particular aim or scheme before she had foisted it on her acolyte. This, for the moment, is was what had happened with the dating site, and would most probably happen with the cheery lad. If truth be told, he was a bit too common to pursue in Katie's opinion, but she loved the brief excitement, always would. His interest was diverting but not much more. There was no hunger in him, only curiosity and the chance of having fun.

The evening was a rich one for David Potts: slightly round and always genial, though not familiar. Many people envied him his situation. He was not a rich man, but he was certainly comfortable, and his material well-being was reinforced by his lack of material wants. That earlier radicalism which had produced the wind-turbines had slowly softened under Margaret's care into a less reclusive and austere manner, hence the corn festivity.

On this evening, he felt like a man complete. Margaret was always thereabouts, listening with sympathy and laughing at poor jokes. Her patience seemed remarkable, but David knew more than to take it for granted. In truth, the culture of the home was more her doing than his. She softened his hard outlines with homemade jams and a sort of demanding patience which kept him from becoming the fanatic he might have been.

At the heart of it was the knowledge that he knew he'd got a good one. There was no man there who did not feel him to be lucky, and looking round himself, at his well-tended farm and greenhouses now full of known friends, he counted his blessings and felt himself fortunate. Even Misty seemed more like her own self, and he had watched in quiet amusement as the cheerful chappy tried his luck with her. In truth, he had few worries on that score. She clearly knew how to avoid trouble, and yet there was a sort of question in his mind, nothing urgent, but a question nonetheless.

He'd met Margaret when he was five. They were not always friends, and girls were useless at lots of things, so what would have been the point in that, but later on, when studies and outlook and music began to matter, she had come more and more into focus until an understanding had developed. He'd never had another girlfriend, and he did not miss the experience. She kept him waiting, but never too long. Somehow, she always seemed a bit wiser than he did or more aware. You take your pick. As a late teenager, he got stuck on ecology, and he remembered banging on about it to his dad, who merely shook his head as he ploughed the artificial fertiliser into his soil.

David was not a radical as such but had opinions not to everyone's taste he was sure, but she was happy to take him as he was, and he had never strayed far from her side. He knew that he'd been lucky, and he wanted his daughter to be the same. He felt Misty was more like him than Margaret. More angular and un-centred, if you follow me, but lovely. Always lovely, without a doubt. Seeing her and thinking that made him smile as he dipped more corn into his boiling pot, but still there was a question on his mind. Where was her other half, and would he be the rock, that Margaret was to him?

By Misty's age, they were already an item and a half. They had not married that early, because David thought it a bourgeois institution, but Margaret had settled that in the end. She wanted children and would not have them out of wedlock, so wedded he was. He had his principles, but they would not make him stupid. Misty never seemed to have a beau. She had friends, and moved around in circles but no one had knocked on her door. Later, I heard through someone else, that the nearest man to perfect that he'd seen was me, but I was already married to his niece. What an irony was that.

What he didn't know about me would shock him, and I made a point of never commenting on her in anything but the most general way. He knew I had an interest in her, and I think he sometimes thought that my interest might be deeper than was recognised, but we never said anything. I had a reputation for being a caring man who put others before his own self-interest. It was a thing about me he liked and trusted, and I had never given him any need to doubt it and never would. That was my solemn promise to him and to myself, unspoken, of course, but serious none the less.

Nothing was certain. Nothing was solid. Life teaches you that, but I had met good and warm people here, and they had given me their trust and welcomed me into their home. To be a part of a community like this was beyond my imaginings, but the twin pressures of my wife's indifference and the beguiling, I might say intoxicating figure before me, were challenging this fragile sense of well-being. I could feel it. I was being consumed by a longing which would only end in chaos and my personal destruction. Somehow I must stiffen my resolve. Feelings, as my father may have already understood, are wayward and full of hidden menace.

~2~

Far away, in Perth, Australia, a man moved to his laptop and had a look to see if he had any messages. There was a curious red heart icon which told him he did. Within the heart was the number '1'. It meant he had one message.

"I Love your poetry. Did you write it?"

He stared at the photo beside the message and felt himself slide sideways. Not literally, of course, but he got a serious sense of displacement. This was a girl who would never look at him twice, but here she was asking a gentle question without artifice or fear. He was beside himself with nerves and wonder, and thought a lot about how to reply. He felt alert and nervous. He realised his response was critical and read her profile searching for a clue. In the main, it was bland and general, but there was a hint of inner softness, possible tenderness, which resonated with him. She seemed slightly 'other-worldly,' if anything. That she, looking at him, was seeing a figure which did not really exist was now forgotten. He was too far into considering her to wonder how his image might appear.

We on this side of the world were mainly deep in sleep, but not I. I was still tossing and turning beside my wife, invoking the 'no-touching' rule as I did. It had never been stated but was understood – a particle of understanding in our complex intimacy. I thought of Misty, of course, and now I was not alone, but I also thought about that girl in the café, and how she had looked at me.

In books and films, people are often good or bad, but in life they are often good and bad. The better part of me, the conscious part of me, wanted to be the man I was thought to be in company: quiet, respectful, and selfless in my way with others. Not some grubby, sneaky guy feeding his secret appetites. I knew I owed it to myself to watch my eyes and thoughts. I could not do that again. The shame of it threatened to drown me in doubts and destroy everything I valued in this little life of mine.

When you got down to it and looked yourself in the eye, it was hard to say who you really were. Like everyone else, I just wanted to survive, day by day, and did what I had to make that happen. But why I wanted to survive, and who was surviving, that was too deep for me.

And what of Misty, who was she, or David, or Geoff or anyone at all? I tried to still myself and regain some composure. One thing was true. Misty was largely unknown to me, apart from smiles, gestures and some verbal mannerisms. We had never had 'the chat.' There were no intimacies at any level, just a whiff of conspiracy built on that look which said 'she got me.' For all I know, it was a mannerism and not a deliberate gesture, but I was too far down the road of longing to think clearly about that any more.

I had read somewhere of people 'projecting' the things they wanted onto other beings. Apparently, it was common on the internet, but in basic human dialogues was that what I was doing? Was I so lonely and isolated that the briefest smile would draw me to create a story? I did not know, but somewhere at the edge of my sleep, I realised that I did not trust my instincts. Within the realm of the emotional I had little sense of what was real.

In his youth, David Potts, I heard from local gossip, was more the angry, opinionated young man, and it was Margaret and his values which had slowly tamed his manner until he became 'a person beyond shallowness.' His good opinion was something I valued greatly, and to lose it would be like the imploding of a star. Geoff... Well, who was he? Practical and patient with his wife, my mother-in-law, and not given to wild statement. He took her vanities in good part, and there was no sense that they were not a couple. He was someone whose respect I valued. All in all, I was a prisoner of my good name. People laughed at my lack of worldliness, but little did they know. These were people I had never seen *in extremis*, but I feared that I was going to if I was not careful. Somehow, in this place of plenty, where I was known and acknowledged as being useful, I seemed to be succumbing to a sense of isolation. Only one thing truly grounded me, and that was sitting by the sea watching the timeless motion of the waves. Like some cosmic heartbeat unmoved by our concerns. In this impersonal but moving landscape I gained some inner perspective. How I need that now.

~3~

Back in Perth, Bernard had had an inspired idea. A brave idea.

He replied, "Yes, I wrote that. I like to write poetry, and I also write songs. Would you like to hear a bit of one?"

It seemed an all or nothing question. Either she would respond positively or silence would descend again. It was still too early to hope, but he would hope anyway. Now he just sat there, looking at her pictures and wondering what she was like. He noted her age and felt slightly uneasy, but who was to say what was right: two souls adrift in life, connecting from a distance and giving comfort to each other, and who might pass a hand of understanding over one another's life? That was just beautiful.

He had no physical thoughts. What moved him was connection and tenderness, and that possibly made his replies sound less intimate. It was emotion he sought more than anything else. That much we certainly had in common. What was his age to them if other things were right? He felt a kinship with her, and allowed himself a fragment of hope.

"What a fool," he thought, but not a fool, really.

When I awoke that Saturday morning, slightly fuzzy and low on sleep, I felt the need to purge and renew myself, so I offered to take Katie out to lunch and shopping. She seemed surprised but not unpleased. Maybe, I thought, her cold manner is a response to mine. Not that I had intended to be distant, but she had accused me of 'always being somewhere else' before. So it was not impossible.

Alright, I thought, let's concentrate, and so I did. Instead of waiting in the shops like other shipwrecked men, who stand somewhere near their wives and wish they were standing somewhere else, I made a point of showing interest and even suggesting clothes which I thought she might like.

Some guy, built like a massive bouncer and normally a figure you would avoid, was sitting outside the ladies changing room and slumped down on one arm. He looked almost like a shipwreck as he wiped his hand across his face. There he was, distraught in this wilderness of dresses, and I felt companionable with him.

As I passed, I said, "It's not all fun, eh?" and sort of laughed.

It was a strange connection but still enjoyable. Much better this than being that furtive man I had been during the week. Katie seemed alight, and twirled and sparkled in various new dresses.

"The blue or the purple, what do you think?"

I looked at her as if this was a question of national importance before saying, "The blue, I think. It picks up on your eyes, and that sweater sits with it so well."

I was driven to this performance by a fear of myself. Misty dimmed into the shadows for me. Re-establishing me with Katie seemed at the heart of avoiding madness.

I realised I had always lived as some sort of guerrilla, filling in and becoming part of the pack, a skilled attendant at some strange event. I did not have the benefit of a temper. I was too watchful for that kind of expression harking back to my old Catholic days. Perhaps what I needed was a father confessor, but then, I had always played a part with them, so not so good a precedent. What I didn't know was how far my experience replicated anyone else's.

How close were Katie and Misty? How close was anyone? It was a question better left unanswered. What I needed to do now was to survive. That's all I had to work with.

In Perth, Bernard had found a way to leave a sound file on his messages, and recorded a couple of verses of his *Love's Outside* song for her benefit. It was all or nothing. He was excited, but not on edge. He'd had a lifetime in dealing with disappointment, so another one would not be hard to handle, and yet he was not unhopeful. What he was sure of was that Derek would have no sympathy with this. Derek didn't do sensitivity, and a women who could not be won over by a decent meal, dress, or smart car was outside his 'hunting zone' as he termed it.

The idea had started with Derek, but the responses were now Bernard's, and he had taken off on his own. His sudden determination and focus would have astonished Derek. More was to come.

Sure enough, when it came, her response was everything he could have hoped for and then more.

"Oh that's beautiful. You have a beautiful soul."

Love takes time to build, so they just stuck to dreams, stoking up the other's sense of what was possible. Shared films followed, and their common list was uncanny. Was this really happening? She asked him to tell her his favourite song and why. That didn't take long to work out. *Somewhere over the Rainbow* sung by Eva Cassidy, so much better than the original in his opinion, and she died of cancer before she even became famous. Both the story and the song were more than moving. On his own sometimes, he might sit and listen to it and wonder if there was a rainbow with someone sitting at the end of it. His capacity for mawkish sentimentality was limitless and how the haunting sound of her voice freed him from constraints.

I'm sure you can imagine what I'm going to say, and you are right, and yes it is incredible. For reasons not dissimilar, she loved the same song too. Misty, had a skill, a knack or however you want to categorize it, of deflecting the real life attentions of men. She knew how to draw your feelings in, as she had mine, and then glide past them, denying all responsibility. She did this so skilfully, I later thought, because she was almost unaware of it herself. Isn't it the case that we often use techniques and exhibit patterns of behaviour of which we are almost totally unaware? I suspect I do.

All this is true, but there was another side to her. Inside her ice chamber, where the maiden sought solitude and peace away from the pressuring expectations of everyone around her, lived a different person. One who dreamed of a soul as tender as she thought herself to be, who could sense the finest nuance in a phrase or moment and feel the same needs in another. It was too remarkable to think of at first, but she felt a sort of conspiracy with Bernard. She kept the contact and her feelings to herself for now, but they charged her outlook and those around her saw freshness in her step, a new optimism, and wondered what could have brought this on.

In Perth, Bernard sat, looking at her response, and finding himself wondering, without practical concern, if this sweet being was who he thought she was. Divided by the time difference and some continents, she was doing the same with him. Both of them, away from prying eyes became hopeless and impractical romantics. Their growing connection seemed a conspiracy of dreams.

The more impractical it was, the more it moved them. For

him, lost in this film script made real life, those troubling details with the wig and hobbies and age dwindled into nothingness against the brilliance of their shared sensibility. She felt the same about herself. Not the falsehoods, because with her there were none, but certainly with the impracticality.

It was too early to say, she told herself, clinging to common sense, but was this man with such a naked and feeling soul the home where she might rest her tenderness?

We might shake our heads. I did mine when I first heard the story, and recall Bernard's addiction to the attentions of Ruby, but perhaps we missed the point. He loved the physical release. Who would not? But most of all, he treasured the connection he felt with her, even if he was mistaken.

With Misty, things were on a different scale, but there was enough common ground to give their emotions room to grow. Both of them, in different ways, were the side-kick, or subordinate of another, and without disclosing that, it was already a powerful common factor. The internet adventure had been started by the mentors, but subtly, and without even realising it themselves, the acolytes had both taken their projects over. In its way, it was a miracle. It was, as I have said, a conspiracy of dreams. I always understood that, but perhaps it was also a tragedy. Only time would tell.

Misty, both at home and college, had always allowed the main agendas of her life to be organised by someone else: either Katie or Carol, and there was no single thing she had ever done which she might say, 'I started this myself.' Her one sign of independence was in her secret. That incident in the cinema, both sickening and disturbing as something she would never discuss with anyone, but in all other matters her life was the product of other people's expectations, beginning with her parents.

Poor old Bernard (am I being too harsh?) was possibly a sadder case than Misty. He had less idea of who he was or what he wanted. He was now old enough to feel or hear the world grumble at him and mutter, "You are surplus to requirements," It was something he was increasingly aware of. He hid deeper and deeper inside himself till the entire fluid larva-like aspects of his life were buried in a bunker to preserve the small portion of him left unmarked by hard experience. How he longed for that sweet girl, who might now have a name, to stretch out across time and miles and calm him with her gentle touch. To hear a voice unblemished by disappointment offer him comfort and soothe away the pain. Make him believe, if that was possible, that the heart and soul of him still had importance. That he was more than a functionary in other people's lives.

Misty, as I have said before, wanted to be an infant teacher and loved all kinds of animals. She loved animals because they might nuzzle you without controlling your behaviour. Their love was neither limiting nor challenging. Young children seemed much the same. In all other areas of her life, as she grew older, she felt somehow strapped in by other's expectations. She had been their plaything and their treasure all her life, and she wanted to be her own person. She was not a rebel, or confrontational, direct, challenging, or anything which might have unsettled Katie or her parents. Always well turned out, but not obsessively so, she stood as the model of what was dutiful and feminine. Without either herself or her minders being aware of it, a prison of expectations had been constructed round her.

Could it be that this sweet, soft voice from another land, with such an ear for the gentle might connect more than she thought possible and be her ally in a demanding world? She was more skilled at sliding past others expectations but not her own wishes. Those were largely unexplored.

Chapter Six

We live in a liberal age where individuals are allowed to create their own chaos, but this was almost a new opportunity for Bernard and Misty. It is something I have some experience of, as you now know, but these two people, almost unaware of their own conspiracy, were just beginning to push at the door. Neither had said a word to anyone else about the connection. Both were sure, and rightly so, that anything they did unannounced would be viewed with the greatest unease as it became known. Both had become perfect acolytes, and acolytes with any sense, do not spring surprises on their mentors, however unofficial the connection. In time, of course, their love would demand a voice and all practical impediments would be swept aside. They feared that moment, and the consequences if they were wrong. At the same time they were excited to be walking this fresh landscape free of outside influence.

Oh, what a field day their friends and controllers would have, laughing at them, and then forgiving them for believing themselves capable of a real and independent life. If things went wrong, making sure the bruises of reprimand they inflicted on their acolytes, with every show of compassion, were marked enough to never be forgotten.

Why do I speak of this with such energy? Because I was little different from them. I was controlled by the whims of Katie, and before her my father. I, too, was an acolyte and a professional one. All my life, I had been like a chameleon surviving by blending into different groups and gaining their trust. It was a thorough skill, developed unconsciously. The only difference this time was I had somehow struck the jackpot. Every paradise has its apple tree, and I was resisting my feelings about Misty to preserve my standing in the community, a place which had become my home and my source of self-respect.

It was early days, but on the internet, early days can be constructed in a minute from a sense of possibility or an email. These dreams can become the centre of a world and shape the needs of the two poor participants until life without the other conspirator can seem impossible. The hard facts were that Bernard was a man on the edge of middle age, with some secret habits which might seem seedy to those of a judgemental nature, and Misty was fresh from college and had neither left home nor held down any kind of job. None of that mattered at the moment. Bernard was darkly aware of the fictions and falsehoods in his profile, but for now, that was ignored. For these few precious moments and days, he would let his feelings engage freely with this other soul and worry about the facts sometime in the future. For now, just discovering each other was all he wanted to feel. To him, Misty seemed a figure sent from Paradise.

While she slept, he looked at her enlarged picture on his laptop, then gave a signal to himself that he was becoming a passenger of his own emotions. Bald, jug eared and slightly lined, he leant forward, clumsily but with purpose, and kissed her pretty image on the screen. In that brief moment of naked honesty, he felt more real than he had ever done before.

Compared to this gentle and newly discovered girl, his ex-wife had been a tyrant and a vixen. Was it possible that such a being as Misty could be for real? For now, as he lay stretched out on his couch, he let his mind float away on pleasing speculations. The obstacles in their path, and there were many, even if all they read was true, only made their situation seem both daunting and more romantic. The higher the peak, the greater the sense of achievement you feel when the summit is reached, and Bernard was already charged with new emotions.

They are not the first people to walk this path or plant this dream in a landscape otherwise barren of promise. It is easier to judge others than yourself. Judging others reinforces identity, but judging yourself undermines your own self-confidence, and mine was frail enough as it was. Perhaps all I will allow myself to say is that I understood their errors far too well.

We talk of qualities like honour, bravery, integrity, and understanding, but when we look in the mirror do we see them in ourselves? So often, they may be in us but as traces in a body also marked by flaws. The further away we are from a person, and the less involved with their daily lives, the easier it is to admire them because our admiration will have no consequences. At this early stage, both parties were free to create a magic out of the other which might not bear the experience of connection. Because of the distances involved, any prospect of meeting initially seemed remote.

Misty, the ice maiden with the warm inclusive exterior, had made the first approach, and therefore felt herself in more control. Each correct response muted her natural caution, filling her heart with something approaching wonder. She sought for affirmation, not for truth.

In Bernard's case he was a veteran traveller, bruised by contact with the outside world, but from this young girl, who in person would never glance at him, he received an innocent interest. His aim was not predatory. He had forgotten half his lies. It was the honesty of his yearning which made the falsehoods in his profile so believable.

Someone would have to make a move. On this occasion, it was Bernard. Something out of character had happened to Derek which was unprecedented and remarkable. Through his work selling IT innovations of doubtful value, he had met a woman slightly older than he was and found himself in thrall to her. His normal courting technique, if you can use that word, had not been employed.

She was the owner of the firm to whom he was offering his services. She ran a large and successful recruitment company, and despite her affectation of dizziness, was nobody's fool. Why she had taken to Derek, I am not sure. I am not saying with certainty that she had taken to him, but she was happy to share his company for the moment. Like him, she was a careless predator and soon saw through his shallow attempts to charm. Far from irritating her, it amused her. There was something else.

Derek, as with Bernard, preferred women who would not seriously challenge or question his standing. He was a pass-master at driving up in his nearly new Mercedes, freshly cleaned, and taking them off to some swankery to dazzle them with his significance. A decent number of these meetings ended up in private behind closed doors, and Derek was satisfied with his technique.

Samantha, as she was called, allowed herself to be taken on a date, and left her actually newer and more expensive car parked at home. More surprisingly, despite his apparent tackiness, she allowed him to glide her to some hotel with an apparently un-missable view, where privacy was sought and intimacies were exchanged. Despite his self-absorption, Derek was uncomfortably aware that this woman was somewhere out of his league and not susceptible to his normal weaponry. Why she was with him was not clear to him, and that unsettled him. He was not comfortable with not having the upper hand. She was with him because his clumsy sophistication amused her for a time. She found his shallow posturing diverting, and she enjoyed being entertained.

As if becoming a new man, he introduced her to his closest friend, a rare thing on its own, and Bernard could soon see this lady was more substantial than Derek's normal quarry. This woman, who was far from unattractive, seemed to enjoy their company. Drinks flowed as details were exchanged.

"And what do you do, Bernard," she enquired: a question which often unsettles all but the stupid.

His reply lacked glamour, but luckily it was only form, and she could hardly have been less interested. To spice things up, Derek revealed that Bernard had been in a band and was a pretty good drummer and song writer. By accident, they had landed on an area of life which still had freshness in her eyes, and she relaxed and looked at Bernard with new interest. She enjoyed mild distractions.

This hotel boasted a grand piano in the lobby, and after prodding, Bernard was persuaded to sit down and perform. This always made him uncomfortable, but he had enough technique to rattle out some chords in a way which suggested there was plenty more where that came from. There was not, but who was to know.

"You're talented," she said, and that impressed her more than wealth. She had enough of that already. Bernard blushed but also felt the pleasure. Derek looked at him with fresher eyes. He'd come up trumps and shown this lady 'with everything,' that they had something to offer her which her money could not buy.

It filled Bernard with dangerous levels of confidence. He became reckless.

"How long have you known each other?" he asked, and was told a couple of weeks.

Yes, they had that freshness, a blend of physical intimacy and lack of personal understanding which marks new courtship in the modern age, but now there was another friendship taking place. For this evening, at least, all outside rules were forgotten, and they were equals sharing a glass of wine.

"I've met someone, too," he said suddenly, warmed by the drink and his new standing, and both Derek and Samantha looked at him.

For Samantha this was a matter of mild diverting interest but to Derek it was an event almost without precedent. Bernard hardly breathed without him knowing so how was this possible?

"What do you mean? How did you meet her?" asked Derek and Bernard told him it was on that internet site.

Naturally, he was not happy to give too much away on first disclosure, so he skipped the fine details saying, "It's early days."

Of course, Derek's search lights were on and scanning the ground for evidence. He was not about to let this one go, although some sixth sense told him he must move carefully. Samantha actually seemed to like Bernard in his own right, which

Derek found amazing, but this regard forced him to treat his friend with unusual respect.

"What's the connection, mate?" he asked, an innocent enough question, but still touched with the irritation that he had not known of her till now.

"It's in the music," said Bernard, pretending to be relaxed.

Samantha seemed to be smiling at him, and welcoming the fact that he might be near this happiness. She had no territorial sense of him and just enjoyed the information at face value. Derek kept his powder dry, but he would find out all he needed to later. Knowing Bernard, the girl would be some nutter who would mess up his already fragile life. There is an understanding on these occasions, and as the evening drew on, Bernard made his excuses and left. Samantha smiled at him with some warmth and said she hoped they met again soon.

~2~

Back in his rooms, Bernard felt conflicted.

Alright, the wine had grabbed him, but this new women was not Derek's normal foil. She was certainly substantial and someone of consequence who liked him as well as Derek. That was a first on its own. Derek's pickups were normally either hard edged materialists or seemingly gullible froth-heads with little interest in someone who lacked 'focus,' another word for wealth. That she liked him was something to store away, and a pleasing boost to his self-esteem. He knew with clarity that Derek would not necessarily be pleased that he had been such a hit, and also be piqued that he hadn't known about Misty.

For a few hours, he still had time for privacy. There seemed only one person with whom he could discuss this new development, and that was Misty herself.

He switched his laptop on and waited for it to boot. A slow process with his old machine, but not to worry, he'd make himself some tea. Soon, with cup in hand, he was staring at her profile, and at that sweet face in which he'd placed such capital. They both new so little about each other, but what they had was real. Of this he felt sure. He started to type.

"I went out tonight, with my oldest friend and his new girlfriend, and we had a lovely time. We ate at a Turkish restaurant, which I think is really good, and then went off to some hotel overlooking the sea for coffee and some drinks. Anyway, you are not interested in that, but I feel the need to share things with you in some way. I told them both about you. I said it was very early days, if any days at all, but that you were someone special. Really special, in my opinion. I told them all about the music, and even played the piano in the hotel. It was kind of magical, really, playing and looking out over the dark blue of the ocean. How I wish you could have been there. Perhaps someday you will be. Should I say that? The strange thing, Misty, is that, to you, I feel I can say anything. It's as if I already know you. Isn't that strange?"

He peered at the message and tried to read it slowly, but it was all too much, and he was sitting there in turmoil.

In the end, he swore under his breath and just thought, "What will be will be."

The message was sent, and the die was cast. Would they face Derek together, at least in some way, or would he find himself alone again? Only time would tell.

It might have been the alcohol, and it might have been his uneasiness when he thought of the impending cross-examination, but he felt both tense and relieved. There was no one else he could tell about this evening. He hoped she'd accept the implied compliment and implied connection. Sleep came slowly if at all. His mind was in a whirl, and he knew, come sometime the next day, that his friend would demand all the answers and might throw mud at this picture of perfection, but for now, it was unblemished.

It was becoming part of Misty's routine now, to switch her computer on and see if she had a message from 'Lemongrass' whom she now knew was called Bernard. The name had sounded a bit old fashioned to her when she first heard it.

Sure enough, that little heart with the number one in the middle of it said all she wanted to know. Her heart did not skip a beat. That is just an expression used by the foolish, but she certainly felt her emotions rise a little as she clicked the button to read. The message was amazing. This gentle man, this sweet boy had given her name a voice in his own country and spoken of her to his oldest friend.

It had not really been discussed between them, because the situation was not fully recognised, but she could imagine what such a conversation with Katie would be like. Even half the tension would be hard to deal with. How brave he was. Almost like a champion. The fact that he had admitted her existence somehow made the whole thing more real. He was announcing their connection. He was waving his little beam of light across the oceans at hers and saying, "It's me. I'm really here."

All this is ridiculous, of course. We all know that. These soggy flights of fancy have no function on their own, but these two dreamers had lost much sense of function. Their conspiracy of feeling was growing more real, and now Misty felt a responsibility to Bernard. She must not let him down. She must tell Katie. The prospect filled her with alarm.

~3~

Something happened at this juncture which took me out of the loop so that, regarding Misty, I heard all the news in retrospect. My father died in the way he would have wanted to: without warning and on the train home from work. A heart attack, apparently. He had not complained of feeling ill or chest pains or of any symptoms of ill-health, but knowing him, this did not mean he did not have them.

Katie and my father, unsurprisingly, had never been close. Possibly on some subliminal level they were too much alike. It is seldom the case that similar people become friends. It is like having two solo trumpet players in a jazz band. Friction is inevitable. That being the case, she was more than happy to let me go off and settle his affairs. She kept her excitement to herself, but her eyes leaked thoughts of money.

Could all her dreams come true? Only time would tell. My father, I now realised, was a confirmed atheist, and disbelieved the permanence of anything which was not either planted in the ground or framed by statute. Affections were always unreliable, and therefore discounted as far as possible. That he was an atheist who brought his son up as a Catholic should not surprise us. I think, in part, it was out of deferred respect for his wife's beliefs and the larger social demands made by his being a significant figure in the city.

He was of an age where a lip service to convention was regarded as important. Now he was dead, it was not necessary to make any such concessions, and it was clear he wanted to be as frank as he could about his opinions on life and the people he had come into contact with. Why he was so angry, I cannot say. He was punctilious about not sharing confidences. His style of parenting was rigorously neutral. I never heard him express much in the way of an emotional opinion. It is possible that he shared some warmth with my mother, and my memories of the time before her death are of a softer figure, but I could well be fooling myself.

He could be convivial at his club or in the office, I am sure, but it was more a means of marketing than a conviction. Through death, he was determined to make this clear. His will was not ambiguous. I was left £500,000 net of tax, with all other monies being donated to some organisation set up to pinpoint the exact location of Atlantis. They received £4,800,000. In some small and obscure way I think it was his way of telling a joke, of saying that life is full of nonsense, and he was delighted to have nothing more to do with it. Needless to say, he did not take me into his confidence, and as he might say, "Speculation without a clear goal is a waste of effort and unlikely to be a productive use of your time."

I was not his executor. That was left to someone at his old firm, who was lavishly rewarded for his efforts. A stipulation was that no one attended his funeral apart from me. I think he dreaded the idea of people uttering sentimental laments over his coffin before drowning their artificial sorrows at his expense. I have no idea, but that is the way it was. He was cremated at the local authority crematorium and his ashes were deposited over his wife's grave – a small note of human emotion. She must have been remarkable in some way. I have little memory of her.

~4~

When I returned home, people were consoling, as you would expect, and I went through all the formalities of showing grief. On the one hand, it is hard to show grief for someone you didn't know, but on the other hand, not knowing your father is a source of grief. It was hard to admit how barren the whole episode had been. How could I make this understood? This bleak, efficient landscape was all I knew as a child, and my new world, the most successful transformation to a new social landscape I had ever made. I had no wish to pollute one with the other and kept my details brief.

Katie, with a thin show of discretion, did not ask me about the will, but you could see that she was ready for any confidences I wished to share. The money was not with me yet. Paperwork moves slower than a snail, but even the knowledge it was on its way somehow gave me more confidence. I had a reasonable living at this time, but I suspect her salary was more substantial. These things were never discussed, but it was the impression I gained. References to my meagre economic resources were sometimes used as part of her belittlement training. I hope I don't sound bitter.

For the moment, I used this new event in my life to seem preoccupied and frowned slightly if she poked at me too much. I could see easily that she was frustrated by this behaviour. Those who cannot control events often become the most detailed observers of them, but as always, I used my father's death as a shield behind which I could preserve a greater independence of thought, my only real capital.

I admit that when asked directly about the will after a few

drinks out with friends had loosened her erratic sensibilities, I lied and said the details had not been released as yet, and I would have to travel back later that month to hear them. In part this might have been to give me peace, but I already knew, however comforting the sum of money was to me, to her it would rank as a significant disappointment. I could do without that now, in the midst of all my personal dramas. Katie had thrown out, almost aggressively, that Misty seemed to have 'acquired a new admirer.' She knew I was fond of Misty, although she took my feelings to be those of a stuffy older brother. That someone of my standing could actually have a romantic attachment to her cousin was too ridiculous to be worth a second's thought.

To be underestimated is an advantage of sorts, and so it was now. In fact, her dismissive view of my attraction to her sex — disregarding her own initial interest in me — was one of the factors which most affected the events which followed. Because when she told me, it was almost as a distraction from my news or out of irritation. You could never be that sure. Her use of language was interesting because it indicated her slight removal from events. It told me clearly that she had not been involved, and it had not pleased her. To give her more unsettling news about my inheritance would have poured petrol on the flames.

I could hear the conversation in my head.

"You really are quite useless, aren't you? Did you never think to pay him a visit or ring him every now and then? What did you expect?"

It will not surprise you to learn that, with Katie, blame always lay elsewhere. I cannot recall a time when she admitted she might have been at fault. The fact that she had never had a good word to say about a man — who probably regarded her as chaos on legs — was never added to the mix.

They met on few occasions, and I still remember my father and David Potts looking at each other at our wedding. For David, at that time, I was already regarded, I think, with some warmth, but also as a sort of refugee. My father was the prison or laboratory I had escaped from. Both images have accuracy I am sure. I am almost embarrassed by my words. "Both images have accuracy," is a phrase straight from my father's lips.

For my father, the cheery eccentricities of my new life, profession, and in-laws were proof that further effort spent on me would be inefficient in thought and deed, and no greater crime existed in his book. Out of some hidden and inexplicable regard for his late wife, he had managed me until I 'achieved majority.' That was his term for being old enough to vote. Thereafter, I was allowed to live my life as I chose, with as little inconvenience to his as he could manage. This would not be said in public, but I think it was true. He would 'note' a shortcoming or example of poor behaviour, but wild assaults on your character as a whole were not something he did. I think he would have regarded such an outburst as vulgar and unnecessary. How he and my aunt had both emerged from the same family circle, I have no idea. It remains one of the wonders of nature.

It is curious how we have these endless debates with people who are no longer in our lives. How we keep trying to explain ourselves to them or justify a course of action long after the person has died or lost all interest in our current circumstances. Even in these early days, I could feel that many questions filled my thoughts in my discussions with my departed father.

One of them was, "Why didn't I have the courage to ask this question when he was alive?"

But we all say that don't we? Half of our heads, as we get older, are full of unfinished conversations. At least mine is. Evidence of madness lies behind the calmest gaze, I have always found. Who knows what events will give it life or expression? In my case, the catalyst was already walking through my life and was the daughter of a man I had grown to admire above all others.

Chapter Seven

It was David Potts, more than Katie, who spoke to me of Bernard, or 'Lemongrass' as David still called him, and who expressed his early fears. He would emphasise the 'e' in 'Lemon' as a way of distancing himself from the situation. It was distressing to witness. I was on one of my visits up there, I think I've mentioned it before, and he started talking about 'this Lemongrass chap, or Bernard, or whatever his name is.' Whenever David became a bit agitated, which was seldom, he often became stiff in his choice of words, and although he disguised it, he was certainly agitated now.

He looked on me as a man of common sense, and it was something I always tried to be. He considered me a man who would not let emotions interfere with judgement. At this time, whatever my private feelings, we were both on the same side. Although David may have had an idea I had allowed my emotion for Misty to grow warmer, I don't think he considered it to be any more than a sort of protective crush and harmless. I am sure a quick tour of my emotions would have shocked him deeply. That is true with most people on most topics, but at this time, as events would demonstrate, David had unbreakable faith in my desire to help him protect his daughter.

Misty was my obsession, and sometimes my thought had threatened to spill over in ways which would have shocked everyone who knew me. 'Offering up these thoughts and appetites to the gods' worked to an extent, but if she was either too sweet or inclusive, or subtly physical, I could feel my sanity leave its moorings. Maintaining that impassive exterior grew harder by the day. To be honest, sometimes I just wanted her, and she seemed to have a weird sense of it. You could almost feel her fanning my flames to the point of conflagration before exiting the room. Was she secretly mischievous? She liked to toy with you, or was it my imagination? It was a skill she had or did not have. To be honest, I neither knew whether I was coming or going. It was compounded by the fact that the next time she came in or saw you, her look would have that general blankness which denied anything had happened. Perhaps it hadn't. Perhaps it was just my fevered imagination, but it still felt real to me.

All this turmoil was unknown to David, who looked at me to 'steady the ship' and introduce a note of common sense and reflection into the dialogue between the two girls. His trust and confidence in me were both humbling and embarrassing. How much I wished I could be worthy of this opinion, and how much I wanted to be.

Katie, like everyone else, had been surprised by the news, and this was not normal for her when it came to Misty. I'm sure it unsettled her, but she hid her surprise behind one of those bright and brittle smiles which would have done credit to her mother. Misty, always canny in my opinion, had announced her news in that fake casual way girls can have when imparting important information. She did it at the café on a Saturday morning, where she and Katie met with village friends. I was hiding behind my newspaper, acting out the resident bore, and no one could see or notice my reaction as Misty spoke.

A torrent of cross examinations followed and, as is the custom on these occasions, Misty brought out the evidence that her new beau was a man of extraordinary gifts and intelligence. He could be anything he wanted, of course, but extraordinary was mandatory. All the girls understood this. Misty, not an academic girl by nature, reeled off some of his poetry and songs which she had already memorised. All the girls gasped at his sensitivity and helped further the sense of wonder that Misty had found herself a true man of stature, a keeper, a companion on life's journey.

In the circumstances, whatever Katie felt, she had to be excited, and she decided she was excited, joining in the general inquisition. Soon, she was talking about the internet site and taking 'ownership' of the whole experience. She slid herself quietly into her normal role as the controller, and I think Misty was relieved to see her friend 'on-board.' At the time, I just read my paper and pretended that her news was of little consequence to me. I found some item about corruption in high places and muttered about it as if it was the chief topic of the day. Being boring was my main line of defence. It was only later, with David, that I approached the subject more openly. We were both concerned.

Later that evening, when Katie and I were alone, I broached the subject again.

"What do you think about this Bernard guy? Do you think we know all we need to know?"

She just looked at me as if to say, "Why should you be worried?"

I answered with, "It's just that David is a little concerned."

That made the matter right. My being concerned would have been far too personal, but my representing David on behalf of those who kill emotion was perfectly plausible, and just drew her normal sigh.

"You just don't get it do you, Bill? Do you know what love is?"

My reputation for emotional blankness had saved me, and I turned to brush my teeth as if the matter was closed for now, but it would never be closed. I had justified my interest, and she could rely on me to be as irritating as normal. My behaviour, at this key moment, had alarmed nobody, and I was grateful for that. I longed for darkness to grant me privacy and allow me to dwell upon events. How serious was it? Had they actually spoken, or what about Skype? I had no firm knowledge at this juncture.

In fact, things had progressed significantly, I found out later.

Bernard had revealed the existence of a sick grandmother who used up a lot of his time and money. This came out because, although he could Skype with Misty, he had no camera as his laptop was too old. Any suggestion that he might be free to travel or buy a new laptop or do anything physical to aid the romance was always explained by the grandmother, but in such a way as to emphasise his frustration.

Oh, how he wished these barriers did not exist, and he could just fly to her side and finally hold his sweet love in his arms. Misty was frustrated but understood. In protection of her first romance and the man who inspired it, she was willing to gloss over any difficulties and find new ways to develop their relationship. By now, Katie was firmly 'on-board,' and the two of them started to work on a plan. As always, when dealing with another's life, Katie's plans were excessive. There was no other way. My confidence that the whole thing would blow over soon disappeared.

Good things had come out of the conversation. He had never been married, worked as a surveyor, and had regular employment; a decent social life, was free of drugs, and not dependant on alcohol. He wrote his music, and together, he and Misty were talking about how to get his stuff on YouTube because, "The world needs to hear your voice," said Misty. Bernard loved to hear her belief in him. It was like water falling on the plains after years of drought.

Katie, of course, was not that worried by the details, or by his singing, which she could take or leave, but she did not make that clear to Misty. What she liked was the drama and romance, and was happy to do anything to keep the dream alive. It was so much more stimulating than her normal everyday routine. In a real sense, the girls became closer and shared the dream together. They shielded each other from more prudent gazes. Especially from David.

My stance was taken to be the same as his, little did they know, and at home, I was dismissed as one who had no real heart and feeling. I was happy to be that man for now.

In Perth, things were not dissimilar. Derek, although more

masculine in his approach, had decided that this liaison was worth pursuing. Any worries that Derek had about his friend's age or hair were brushed aside. That he was the author of these falsehoods was of no interest to him. They were a marketing strategy. They either worked or did not. It was never a matter of great consequence to him.

A suggestion by Derek that Misty might be persuaded to send over a picture of herself in a bathing costume – or not a bathing costume – was ignored by Bernard. He was not going to suggest that to Misty under any circumstances.

In truth, the dialogue between Bernard and Misty remained remarkably gentle and unspecific. Yes, there were more and more kisses and wild expressions of increasing devotion, but nothing sexual was ever said. Misty loved that about him, and for Bernard, her innocence was a big part of her attraction. This strange coincidence was at the heart of their romance. A tragic undercurrent moved beneath the surface. The more their love grew, the more he lied to protect it. At heart of it, quite possibly, Bernard believed that she would never have looked at the real forty-two-year-old baldie with two daughters, and who are we to doubt his judgement?

In time, things became a bit more physical, and he might talk of running his hand down her back, or she of leaning into him and feeling the warmth of his chest, but it had not gone any further. Both were shy and frightened of shocking the other. It remained a conspiracy of inexperience, which frustrated Derek but left Katie unmoved.

All the time, I was discussing the situation with David, and we were both growing increasingly concerned at developments. The momentum was clearly with the relationship, and there seemed to be little we could do to stop it. David, once in my presence, had had the 'What do we really know about this guy' talk with Misty, but it just made her uncomfortable, and he was warned off further pressure by a look from Margaret. I was there, a witness to his developing unease.

What I did not know, at this time, was that Misty and Bernard discussed the whole thing together all the time. At around midday in her time, it was evening and after work for Bernard, and they had taken to talking to each other pretty much daily. Any sense that their love was under siege brought them closer together. They would find a way. Misty, amazingly, was keener than Bernard, because she had nothing to hide. Oh yes, his feelings were painfully genuine and dominated his waking thoughts, but the details concerning his age, hair, and the nonexistence of a grandmother were yet to be resolved. The prospect made him nervous.

He was nervous of anything which would bring him into sharper focus and expose the falsehoods, but these events have a momentum of their own. To be too uninvolved would have risked losing everything, and he could not bear the thought of that. This connection had brought him as much happiness as anything he could remember.

"Get her over here," said Derek. "Once she's on our home turf, what's she going to do? It's that simple."

Misty offered him her love and hinted that, if they were together, she would 'offer herself' to him. The thought made Derek squirm, but also made him hunger for her. In that, he had my sympathy. It seemed to be a trick of hers: to promise everything before vanishing. I was never sure if I was imagining things. In the end, I am only talking about looks and glances, and sometimes casual movements of the hand. Perhaps in his case, her promises were more specific. I was not there to judge. Both of them felt the pressure of their romance building between them.

What I did hear, through David, was that Misty had applied for a passport. It was disturbing, and unusually single minded of her in our opinion. There is nothing so frightening as the sight of someone whose progress is always considered and pliable giving into reckless spontaneity and a show of ungoverned determination, and this was Misty now. David could be seen to be going further into himself as he fretted over the future of his beloved daughter. Of all the twists and turns that fate might offer, this had never been on the menu. He'd hardly heard of internet dating and could not imagine it being taken seriously, let alone people travelling half-way round the world to chat with each other. He felt he couldn't probe too deeply, but he wondered about a man who would encourage a girl to travel so far on her own, without first talking to her father.

"What do you think we should do, Bill?" he asked me, and I wished I knew.

In my own way, I was as distraught as her father. With Bernard in her sights, she had been less inclusive of me. No more touching or hinting at a special connection. Clearly, she was saving all her thoughts of intimacy for her internet friend. We, that is, David and I, could only hope that something emerged to make her think again, or that she would just lose interest. What made it worse was the more distant she became, the more I found myself longing for her. I caught myself staring at her more than once in a way which was far from neutral. Her body fascinated me. My secrecy and hunger disgusted me. The more I wanted her, the more David seemed to cling to me and use me as his sounding board when voicing his distress. I could feel myself getting further into trouble. Detachment was everything.

~2~

"All my life, I have been waiting for this moment to arrive."

The words could have been written for Bernard. Tentative, uncertain, and even slightly bewildered as he found himself to be but now the recipient of a women's first, fierce, and independent love. Misty had faced uncertainty and difficulty at home from her father, so he'd heard, but nothing had stopped her growing closer to him and declaring herself more and more committed.

She had even said to him, "Our love will not be denied." It is not easy to hear those lines with a straight face, but Misty said them.

Perhaps there is nothing as dangerous as a cynic converted to the rush of uncluttered innocence. It was scary and humbling, but also unsettling. There was still the small matter of the 'misunderstandings' about himself. A long-term relationship might demand he should come clean about his 'intentions,' but it was growing ever harder to broach the subject.

For Misty, this was her first experience of allowing her happiness to be controlled by another so intimately. For Bernard, things were slightly different. He was now forty-two years old, and it was a long time since anyone had looked on him as being 'full of promise' or the coming man. His musical ability had gained him some attention from casual judges, but he had received no professional recognition. His job paid some bills but little else and was free of glamour or street credibility. It was just a job.

Once, when he was in his late thirties, some wise-cracking office junior had asked him, "How old where you when you first discovered a passion for quantity surveying?"

It had brought a laugh from people in the office, but there was no passion in the occupation. For most people, it was a job you drifted into and not a vocation. Almost anyone with a sense of order and some mathematical ability could manage the responsibilities as long as they could handle the boredom. Bernard managed it, but he now knew his place as one of life's 'also rans,' office fodder, part of the crowd. However you describe it. There is a lot of talk, these days, of people 'finding their direction,' focusing on their goals, having a clear objective, discovering the inner you. Of each man or women having their special place in the universe and position on the mountain top. Of life being a voyage of self-discovery. I could go on, but there is another sense of life.

That is why we plant far more in the way of seeds than we expect to see in plants. Not all seeds will germinate. That there is more talent and ability in the world than will ever be discovered. That 'recognition' is not a divine right.

Bernard was in that place in his life when he had begun to wonder if, in the big scheme of things, he was surplus to requirements. That any unique ability he possessed might also be claimed by another who, by accident of birth or circumstance, happened to be nearer the top of the food chain. You get my drift, I'm sure. Many people divert themselves with ill-focused dreams until they find themselves entering middle age with no progress in their lives, and something of a mess behind them. For Bernard, with one ex-wife and two children aged twelve and ten, the sense of 'new adventures' seemed someway behind him.

Don't get me wrong. In his yearning and longings he was ageless. Can we say timeless? He had a knack of articulating regret and isolation in his songs, which people enjoyed as long as they didn't have to pay to listen to them. He was a decent, honest man on many levels, but somehow he had landed himself in a mess, albeit one from which he received the most tender attention he had received in his whole life.

He knew more than anything that he should come clean. Misty was talking about their meeting up. Apparently, she had applied for a passport. She told him all this with much excitement, but each new progress was making him nervous. He wanted to be loved by her more than anything and found he just didn't have the courage to tell her the truth. He was left praying for a miracle. She was the first and only person to have identified with and believed in him so fiercely, and the one he had lied to most. The irony was not lost on him.

Derek had another point of view. "What's the point of worrying? Either she comes or she doesn't."

Frankly, Derek regarded the whole thing as amusing. If she arrived, took one look at Bernard, and got straight on the plane home that would be a story to remember. It's not impossible that he felt piqued that Bernard had advanced the adventure so far without him, and he might gain some pleasure from the whole thing descending into farce. What a great story that would be. He would dine out on that for years.

"Do you remember when that young girl came from England, took one look at Bernard, and left on the next plane?" The comic possibilities were endless. Derek was not without compassion, but it was largely limited to himself.

Two things had happened. Bernard had made a decent impression on Samantha, with whom Derek was slightly smitten, and recently she had remarked, "Sometimes you could be a bit more like your friend Bernard. He actually cares about people."

To be compared with Bernard unfavourably was unheard of as far he was concerned. He found it hard to grasp that, for a woman who had more wealth than Derek could pretend to, 'genuine' qualities were often harder to find than a display of material abundance, and she had found some in Bernard. She was not aware of his lies, or the girl's age or other details which might blemish his character. She could not mistake how genuine his feelings were, and how little avarice or 'show' there was in him. That made a pleasing change for her. That Derek had the friendship of such a man was one of the things which kept her with him, although his charms were now seriously fading.

To Derek, telling the truth was a marketing gambit, and not something to aspire to. Should Bernard actually be able to slide past any sense of falsehood and 'have his way' with the girl, that, too, would make a grand story on its own. Derek would be happy to enjoy taking a decent share of the credit whatever the outcome. Let's be honest, he would be happy to take a share of the girl as well, but sadly that might not surprise you.

To me, despite the dangers and my own unease, Misty remained a pure, sweet, and innocent being with just the right degree of charm and 'knowingness' to keep your attention. To Derek, she was little more than a scalp, and he had no time for moral niceties. Such an activity would be pathetically naive in his opinion, and who would I be to argue with his approach. To date, it seemed to have gained him everything he wanted.

"It's winners and losers mate. Don't over complicate things too much," was Derek's standard line.

His approach did little to influence Bernard at this stage. Even Derek could see that his friend was in the grip of new and strange emotions, but what Derek achieved was comforting Bernard about his lack of candour. Bernard felt with men he must be a man, even if in private or that small seat at the film theatre he might admit to other things. It was clear, even to Derek that this whole episode was something new, but surely the game was just the same. Apart from the ribbing, he did his best to keep his friend on track, and his eye on the main prize. What else would you expect?

For both of them, used to life in the big city, with all the choices and complexities it offered, it would have been hard to understand how different was the life of a village girl from the other side of the world, even if they had bothered to think about it. The relationship was about internal values and not external realities. Very little talk between the two parties was about the experiences of their everyday lives.

Something had happened to Misty. Something no one would have ever considered possible for a person so mild and pliable. She had discovered determination and steel of purpose. On this subject, she had become difficult to deal with. Men have died or thrown themselves to lions for their beliefs, so this stance may not seem as extreme to you as it did to me, but I still found it hard to handle. My sweet and gentle Misty, with that delicious and unsettling promise of intimacy and, dare I say it, raw sexiness, was now much more directed. Do you see how I called her 'my Misty'? How stupid I was becoming.

David was very disturbed, but his 'light hand on the tiller approach' to child rearing was not suited to these more stormy waters. I think he vented his worries with me and certainly with Margaret, but otherwise kept them to himself. Misty now had a picture of Bernard on her bed side table. There seemed, to my eyes when she showed me the photograph, something a little odd about the hairline, but I was not brave enough to notice it in her presence. What I did know was that her passport was now ordered and would be here within a month. Then, to coin a famous phrase, the cat would be well and truly among the pigeons. What would happen then? Was she really ready to go off and see this man alone – a girl whose longest trip away from her birth locality was less than 200 miles?

~3~

Bernard, as I have intimated before, was one of the most innocently destructive people you might meet. His wife, vilified to anyone who would listen to him, was, perhaps, not the villainess he portrayed her to be. To be honest, any husband and father who engaged in paid extramarital sex and researched pornography on the web would be likely to irritate the woman who shared his home.

Now he seemed to be doing it again, but once more, he had not fully grasped the position he was in. Because much of his motive was sincere, he thought the odd inaccuracy could be forgiven. What he failed to understand was that these minor discrepancies had become much more than details. Like all perpetual liars, he was used to deluding himself. He did it without noticing.

He was more than dimly aware that some kind of reckoning was on the horizon. Misty, who was now acting more like a virgin warrior, and who wore his colours on her heart, was talking of their first meeting. She understood his difficulties. She admired him beyond words for the way he looked after his grandmother, and she would do the running. It was a small price to pay for joining herself with him. On reflection, her tone seemed edged with hysteria. The irony is that Bernard certainly had great sensitivity of soul. The problem was it was unconnected with all other areas of his life.

Back at home, there was another person involved in these events. Margaret was one to keep her council and only speak when it was clearly necessary. David always listened when she did. There are those, or most of us, who talk more than we think and others who think more than they talk. Margaret was one of those. She was a person who coped from the background. She still remembered the first time she had seen David, as he squatted on a path in the school playground.

"What you doing?" she had asked in her young girl's voice. She was only five, and he pointed with a twig at some snail crossing the path. "What you doing?" she repeated to his concentrated silence.

He said, "Helping it."

No one would really understand what he meant. Was he imitating the action of the 'Lollipop Lady' who stopped the traffic as they crossed the road to school, or just showing curiosity or both? Even at that age he had an eye for, and an interest in, details. It was the little things he noticed. In time, these might turn out to be the big things, but that is a more adult perspective. Margaret was too young to understand all this, and so was he, but there was a manner of isolation and caring about him which intrigued her unformed character.

At that young age, there was no stigma to having a girl as a friend. That would come later when playing with dolls was not a proper pastime. For now, they were just two young beings sharing curiosities. Margaret was three months older than David, and as such, took on the more mentoring role. She organised his relations with real life in ways which amused both sets of parents. In this small place, the parents knew each other, and there was little mystery. Steve and Betty, her mum and dad, ran a bakery in town and were plain and kindly folk as far as was known. That is, they did not challenge the sense of public order and joined in village ceremonies. I had met them, at the 'Cornfest' and on other occasions, but only to exchange pleasantries.

What matters is that these two always stayed in touch, even at an age when those of a different sex were just not acceptable, and a trust built up between them. I will not bore you with the details of their romance, but it was one of those phenomena which restore your faith in the simple and the beautiful. A detail worth recalling might be that things reached a stage where both sets of parents hoped 'things might progress' and were mightily pleased when the engagement was announced.

I remember David saying once, out of the blue, "Art is not good mannered. It is about understanding without fear. Of seeing as far as you can see without protecting yourself from the view." From any other person, in any normal household, such a remark might have prompted a response, but with her, he was free to act and think as he liked, and she with him. It was one of his longer statements.

Their union was based on a wide area of understood and common values. There was no cause for heated discussions. David might have some theories which might appear eccentric, but Margaret kept her council and never ridiculed his point of view. She always had an eye for what was substantial and knew, behind his odd manner, beat the heart of a decent and caring man. He had never given her any cause to question him. Such stories are uncommon, and more so in an urban landscape where each life seeks its own destiny in a conscious expression of ambition. She was content to be at home, and kept herself busy with the domestic activities, and helping David when it mattered. The home was her expression and its well-being her achievement. She had no need to prove herself. It seems a dated set of values, but they still worked for the Potts.

Only on those occasions when David got a bit heated did Margaret stir herself. She was no saint. Let's not get carried away. Her figure had rounded to a pleasant shape and exercise was something taken by accident, but her thoughts were generous and kindly. That was her central characteristic. Something else about her, which I soon understood, she was one of those beings who is instinctively wise. I don't know how you describe it. She had a good sense of balance. If she made a point it would be a foolish person who discounted it. None did in her circle. I was an admirer of hers, you may have gathered, and as far as I know, she liked me. She had no obvious reason not to, and long may that continue I kept saying with more and more desperation.

In the main, they were a couple who were fortunate and unfortunate. They had found each other early, loved, valued, and trusted each other without thinking, and lived harmoniously on the proceeds of a business, which happened to be economically sound. It was much more a case of luck than judgement, but that is often the case. How often do we find ourselves taking credit for something we did without realising its importance at the time? More centrally, what their life had not taught them was how to deal with difficulties outside their centre of influence.

Now in the drama and romance of Misty and Bernard such an event had arisen. Misty was starting to act without thought for others – an unprecedented occurrence. It was hard to come to terms with. David was saying very little, then a lot and very little, but what he was not doing was dealing with the situation very well. It distressed Margaret to see him act like this. In all their years, she had not seen him this stressed, and she thought deeply about ways to help him.

Once or twice, she had spoken herself with Misty when no one else was in the room. The bond between mother and daughter was as deep as these things can be, but even she found Misty unusually stubborn on the subject. Misty was in love, that much was clear. Some deeper part of Margaret understood, for reasons which were not clear, that Misty needed to be in love, and the object of it was of secondary importance. Something in this man had allowed Misty to set her feelings free and that was the end of it.

You may have seen someone you love and value lose their temper. Swear at you and curse the world at large. The wisest among you will acknowledge that there is a period when your friend or lover is controlled much more by their passions and emotions than by reason, and trying to discuss things in an orderly way is wasted breath. Margaret was in that situation with the two people whom she cared most for on this earth. Nothing was being said, as such, but Misty was having her chat with destiny, or however you characterise it, and her father was beside himself with anxiety. Time would provide a solution. It normally did. Even she had some doubts but knew better than to voice them. She waited for her moment, and calmed her family with meals and routine.

Misty, a normally slightly scatty girl, full of harmless whims had now become more reclusive and spent much of the evenings in her room. She did not seek her parent's approval or understanding or introduce her man to them – all the things you would have expected. My theory was that somehow this was a continuation of the incident in the film theatre. Possibly, she was trying to re-establish the innocence of men in her eyes, and Bernard was her vehicle. I'm not a psychologist and do not pretend to have the answers, but it was the theory I settled on in the end. Somehow, Bernard's lack of physicality and his artistic, naked sensitivity were so different to the plodding and predictable approaches of other men around her and so contrasted to that ungoverned and primal attack she had suffered in the cinema that he became the balm she sought. If anything, his need of her and his lack of demands made her feel more in control. We could go on forever with our theories, but where will that get us, apart from living with anxiety? That's all they did, Margaret and David, as the situation moved beyond their understanding.

You know how it is between people who are comfortable with each other. More is known than said. So it was with these two, who one evening were sitting up in bed reading their respective books, and trying to be interested, when Margaret said, "I've had an idea."

"What is it?" said David, who knew to listen if Margaret had an idea. Her 'ideas' where seldom trivial.

"How would it be if we helped Misty get to Australia to see this boy, on the understanding that she takes Katie and Bill with her? We know Bill can be trusted to keep an eye on her and make sure that nothing stupid happens. I think we might be able to get her to go along with that."

There was a pause while David reflected on her statement, then he put down his book and leaned across and kissed her. "What would I do without you?" he said. "It's more than brilliant. Bill will keep us posted, and we know he has a soft spot for her. He would never let her come to any harm. She listens to him, as well."

The atmosphere in the bedroom had lightened. Now they had a strategy. It might be that, when we all went over, I would tell them that the boy was really a good sort. Perhaps – and they did not want to get carried away – the boy might entertain the idea of moving to England and joining them in running the farm, or at least in working from the village. If he was not suitable, they would trust me to settle the matter. I did not seem to be without influence, and even Katie listened to me when I was serious.

Having settled on a plan, they knew it was all about timing. David was more than happy to leave his wife to make the suggestion. She would pick the moment as she always did.

Chapter Eight

Sometimes you don't know how worried you have been until the tension eases from your shoulders. Sometimes you don't know how your general demeanour has been affecting everyone else. That was the case with David. Of course, he was still worried. He was still concerned that his daughter was in the middle of making a crucial and damaging mistake, but now he felt a lot more secure. At this stage, I had no idea that he wanted to involve me in his plans.

To be honest, if she were to go off to this musical and sensitive being in Australia, and out of my life, I would feel pain and loss, but at least I would not suffer constant temptation. It was a rational point of view. I had made significant efforts to build bridges with Katie in the way of shopping trips and meals, and it seemed to be having some effect. My greater attentions to Katie had been met with initial bewilderment and suspicion, but she had gradually eased her manner towards me and my domestic situation became calmer.

Through Katie, I was kept up to date with progress, or I heard it from other sources, and it seemed that Bernard was declaring his love for Misty without ambiguity and at the same time urging caution.

"It's a long way to come to find you've made a mistake. Do you think you ought to wait a bit until we are both more sure about everything?"

"But I am sure, darling, aren't you?"

You can guess the dialogue without my spelling it out, but it was the normal push and pull of new-met lovers: at one and the same time questioning each other and re-declaring their commitment.

The hard fact was that Bernard, whatever the truth of his situation, was now too dependent on her warmth and caring to cast it casually aside. He was evasive with Derek, only confirming that 'things were going well' and otherwise kept progress to himself. The only real sign of any new value in his life was that he was no longer seeing Ruby. She was on his mind, of course, but not in his wallet. He thought of her, and even missed the connection. With her, he had a much more open relationship. She knew all there was to know, and still she cared for him on some level. She sent him regular texts saying she hoped he was well, which might have been expressions of genuine interest, or an exercise in marketing. Whatever the motive for their creation, they gave Bernard some comfort, but he would not see her. To do so would have been a betrayal. It is curious how the dissolute can be so scrupulous in certain matters.

When people say, "Let me be honest with you," they mean what they say, but do they know what they are saying? At the most basic level, we know what 'facts' are. We can tell the difference between a tree and grass, or a lion and a giraffe for instance, but can we tell the difference between what we think we feel and what we do feel? I'm not sure. When I speak of being more in control of my feelings, it is hard to say whether I was or was not.

There are many people who have a practical attitude to life. Who are, like a certain kind of camper: happy to find a campsite which has all the amenities they seek and that is the end of the search. For other people, there is no perfect site. They spend their entire trip half putting up their equipment before deciding that the river is too far away or the camp is too near or too far from the road. In fact, there is no perfect site, and they are not willing to accept this.

These are the restless trekkers who wander through life, disturbing the scenery of others in the search for their own perfection. They often never find it, and their pasts are littered with their failures. I was one of these people, and the profile saddened me. I have not mentioned it before, but prior to Katie, there was a string of girlfriends who all may have made acceptable wives for a man less critical than I. Each one was found wanting in some particular, and I kept wandering through the social landscape, leaving traces of chaos behind me until I met Katie.

With Katie, I experienced a sense of purpose, and that restlessness in her, which suddenly meant I was the stable one. The person with a fixed image, and it was a role which pleased me. In that guise, I had moved down, mingled with, and settled in her community. In hindsight, I wonder if I was as much in love with my new persona as the women who had inspired it. Anything is possible.

Thus if I say, "Let me be honest," what I mean is I wish I could be honest, but I don't know myself well enough to be so. Oh, I can answer yes or no to the trivial questions.

"Have you ever been unfaithful?"

Answer: "No."

"Have you ever stolen money?"

Answer: "No."

But when the questions get deeper, they run into my doubts. Was I one of those people who long for peace and cause chaos in their search for it? Who wipe their hands on the clean clothes of the innocent in the search for a purer life? I can say, if that is possible, that I did not seek to harm anyone, but I have to admit that I have damaged others in my past. There was a part of me which would have truly shocked my new community, and it disturbed me when I recalled it. I prayed I had left that part of my life behind.

Was I really like some social werewolf who could never see the moon rise without fearing his own nature? I found the gentle innocence of Misty irresistible, but the undercurrent of some physical awareness unsettled me. Was I really that dull and upright man that everyone respected and who irritated his wife with his lack of imagination? Who freed himself from personal appetites and offered them to the gods rather than succumb to temptation? Or did I just want to be that man?

I fear this final statement may be nearer the truth. Believe this, please: I wanted it to be true more than I can say. I was exhausted by previous adventures and still gained nourishment from this new role I'd found. To throw it all away in some burst of 'self-expression' would be the saddest thing imaginable. Where else would I find such a community as this, or people who loved me as I was, or thought I was. I was exhausting myself with micro-reasoning.

When I looked at David, he was the man I wished to be. Yes, he was restless and seeking for perfection, but largely in the world of ideas and aesthetics. He was what I would call a practical romantic. He had ideas beyond the ordinary, and some of them seemed to be beyond reason, but in the central areas of his life – marriage, work, and travel – he was not restless. He had found his campsite almost without looking, and in that way, was a man to look up to with every fibre of your being. I think I can honestly say that David was the man I most admired, and whose life I most wished to imitate.

Sometimes we might sit there of an evening with 'the girls,' that is Misty, Katie, and Margaret, and we would eat one of Margaret's steak and kidney pies. They were always as near to perfection as I could judge, and David echoed this belief. We would punctuate our chewing by grunting our affirmation and nodding our approval as we savoured the developing range of flavours in our mouths. In this we were like simple men who had nothing to worry about other than food or the design of some artefact. David really was that man. I just wished to be and acted the part.

As always, at the beginning, I believed that I had landed on the perfect camping site, and set about unpacking my character and erecting a future for myself. It was only after the first enthusiasm had passed that I realised the tent I was in was not as perfect as the tent next door, and wondering if anyone would notice if I swapped them. That period of celebration had passed to a degree.

Oh, I knew that I was blessed. I knew I had friendships here which would take a lifetime to discover, but in the middle of this paradise stood Misty with her haunting and unsettling basket of fruit and that look which said, 'one bite will not harm you.'

I would never stop at one bite. There was no image of paradise I had not destroyed by devouring it. Why would this place and life be any different?

I was discovering the greatest fear you can have is of yourself. That no place you visit can be beautiful if you lose control of yourself while you are in it. That in the mirror, the reflection you see is of a man both tame and wild, and both parts are vying for your attention. The awareness of my failings and my hunger had been slow in coming, but now, when all else around me seemed to be welcoming sunshine, I felt the full force of my needs and that destructive restlessness which I thought I had left behind me some years before. Only in the impersonal beauty of the scenery I walked through, or the movement of waves upon the shore did I sense any peace. Only in the tread of men going about their business and locked within unquestioning routines did I find some sense of order. It was fleeting, but how I needed that peace to wrap me in some blanket and grant me sanctuary from my appetites.

~2~

Misty seemed to be a different person these days. Of course, she was just the same as always but to the 'micro observers' like me there was something more directed about her. More focused. She had a mission, and she was not going to fail. That mission was to see Bernard and give him the comfort and understanding his poems and songs so eloquently longed for. Some of him remained foggy, of course, but his essential and naked vulnerability was what drew her to him.

All her life she had been, to a large extent, the perfect daughter and good acolyte. Nothing she had done in her twenty-two years had given those who loved her any concern, and she had no wish to do so, as far as I knew. She was not a rebel, or one who seeks her own voice in the world. To date, playing with her small stock of farm animals and Spotty the dog and a number of cats, plus those few small children she came into contact with seemed enough, but now she had received a new and slightly different calling.

A man needed her. He did not want her, make demands on her, or express animal lust. He was just vulnerable and sensitive in a way the world has trouble accepting. That was clear to Misty. He had a talent, it seemed to her, that was far above the ordinary. She would not let him down.

She did not want to upset or offend her parents. No two people could matter more to her than they did, but in time they would grow to love Bernard as she did and welcome him into their family. Her daydreams had gone that far. Away from the curiosities of her friends and even Katie, her flights of fancy had advanced the romance a long way down the road. Their first kiss was a long way over, and even physical intimacies had been gently played with. She was ready to be a woman.

She had told Bernard that she was coming to see him. As always, he had been endearingly awkward about the idea, and said that she might 'waste her time travelling over that distance to meet him, only to be disappointed,' but she knew her man. For him, she wanted to ensure that 'love was not outside' to misquote his song.

Most women would settle only with a man who was not afraid to be a man. Who clearly wanted them emotionally as well as physically, but Misty had had enough experience of being wanted physically, although no one in her circle knew that. Being wanted and being replete emotionally was the natural inheritance of a loved daughter in a stable home. She had no sense of being neglected or under appreciated. Always cherished to the point of suffocation, she wanted a chance to cherish someone of her own who did not purr or was young enough to pay with toy soldiers or dolls. Her time had come. Destiny had called from across the world, and she would not deny it.

To those of us more bruised or circumspect, her naivety might seem misguided. We might stretch that to appalling, but her feelings were always genuine. Who can sneer at that? Her father, rich in eccentricities, somehow had a good sense of what was real and possible. He might be viewed as being on the outer fringes of what was 'normal' to many people, but when it came to his family, friends, and livelihood, this oddly dressed 'tree-hugger' could be as wise as anyone and more than most. Add to that the presence of his wife and you are left with a formidably powerful and grounded couple. Appearances really can be deceptive.

The evening came when Misty sat down with her parents. It was slightly late for them to be having a 'significant' conversation, but she had just finished talking with Bernard whom she could not see, but the sound of his piano playing and his latest song: "It's not that easy for a man to realise, The love he seeks to find there is just not in your eyes," was too powerful to ignore. In truth, it was not his latest song, and had been written over twenty years before, but she was not to know that. The hard facts were that, torn between guilt and a longing for her understanding touch, he had lost his creative edge and had no new material to play her. In the scheme of things, it was a small deception.

"Dad," she said without preamble, and who would not be impressed by her new maturity and sense of purpose, "I have to go and see him."

"I knew you were going to say that," David replied, and his ease of manner surprised his daughter. She had no idea how many weeks of anxiety, conflict, and conversations with her mother had led him to this final sense of ease. He added, "We are willing to pay for your flight, and you go with our blessing, and we have only one request."

Misty could not have been more surprised. She had been dreading this 'talk' for some time, but it was turning out to be the easiest chat imaginable.

"You take Katie and Bill along with you, just so your mum and I know you are safe. Bill will look after you, but won't interfere. You know that."

To be honest, on a pedestrian front, the fare had presented a formidable obstacle to the romance, so that piece of news was very cheering. And the presence of Katie and myself… Well, part of her was relieved not to be alone. She had absolute faith in Bernard. He was a gentle and giving man who would never harm her, but she had never been overseas, and having trusted companions with her made the whole scheme more approachable.

David then added, "I haven't asked them yet. I didn't want to ask behind your back, but I am sure they will agree."

The irony was, even among the three of them, that Katie was an unavoidable part of the deal, but my stable, even-handed, and selfless maturity were what was most required. They all considered me as being a man who could ensure the right thing happened without being heavy-handed. How I had been able to create such a reputation for myself is hard to fathom, but I had. That boring, predicable being I became in daily company had a role, and that was clearly needed now.

Despite the hour, and now lost in anticipation, she insisted on ringing Katie and asking us to go over to the farm immediately. As soon as the phone was put down, I could see something was afoot. Late night drama with a hint of urgency. What could appeal more to my wife?

Without even explaining the nature of the call she just said, "Don't just sit there, we have to go over and see Misty now."

Katie in full flow is a hard person to resist, and soon we were in our car and off for the seven minute drive to the farm. I said nothing, of course, but Katie kept conjecturing and creating whirls of excitement, which meant all I had to do was nod or say yes every now and then. Being boring is not hard work, but behind my dull exterior, I was full of the same questions.

As we walked through the door, Katie was consumed by tingling anticipation and shot glances at Misty who was herself almost translucent with excitement. I stared at her briefly with wonder. I had rarely seen her look more beautiful, but soon I collected myself and turned to David with a friendly nod.

Before we had sat down, David said, "I won't keep you in suspense. Misty has been chatting away with her young man and has finally decided that she has to go over to see him. I think this is right and proper, but given the distance and the uncertainties, both Margaret and I would be much happier if you both joined her on the trip."

"Oh, yes, of course," said Katie without thinking and then rushed over to give her friend a hug.

Normal service had been resumed and my excitable wife was allowed to be excitable and left me to say, "It's always a pleasure to help."

My private thoughts were of another colour, but for now a welcome sense of shock and numbness was taking me through the conversation.

As far as Katie was concerned, we had to go. My acquiescence was taken for granted. I am sure that she would much rather be going alone with her friend, and they had been free to indulge in the full adventure of this new romance together, but the fact that my presence might be welcomed by the parents was somehow understood. Don't get me wrong, she would welcome the presence of a boring foil like me, as long as I didn't try and ruin anything. I understood her, but the kind of ruin I dreamt of was very different from her own imaginings.

I understood immediately that, for David and Margaret, I was the principal companion, and that they trusted my stable presence to ensure that nothing bad happened to their daughter. Despite the pain I would be put through, I was moved by their trust and promised myself that I would perform to the highest standards. Here was a clear, unvarnished opportunity to be the selfless noble being I so admired and wanted to be.

I looked David in the eye and said, "I'll look after her for you," and I saw the look of recognition and trust which he returned. It was one of the finest moments I can recall, and showed how far I had come in establishing myself as a man of understanding and values.

I swore to myself that I would be everything her father expected of me. I gloried, for a few dizzy and illusionary minutes, in the idea of myself as some medieval purist who values truth more than gain, nobility more than desire. I could go on. Even the denial of my secret longings made the experience richer as I basked in the heightened sense of being an admired man. It makes me feel ill as well, but at that time, I really believed that I might become that person and those gross errors of my past would be nothing more than shadows, that unsettling episode at the café but a brief setback.

Katie was beside herself with excitement, and full of plans for the adventure, and in the car home warned me 'not to spoil anything,' whatever that might mean, but to Misty somehow, I got the idea that my presence was a relief.

It's only a theory, but I feel that she wanted this to be her own experience and not to have Katie take it over. There was never an occasion when she would want to cause her parents distress, and though, for many, David's condition might have been seen as overbearing to a girl of twenty-two who was already a college veteran in this small community, that extra sign of caring is what many of them expected. Margaret said little, but you could sense her satisfaction. In many ways the quiet controller, she was delighted to see how successful her compromise had been.

In bed that night, in the hours which had been assigned to sleep, I lay there staring at the ceiling, alternating between a sense of warmth and pride in David's trust in me and fear at my own emotions as I saw Misty wrapped in another's arms. How I would get through that I had no idea. Until I was faced with such a stark image, the pain of my feelings for her had never been so clear. Offering up my longings to some unseen and undefined being high above was a noble aim, but not one easy to achieve.

Misty, radiant and on the edge of getting to see her man, of experiencing womanhood with one who both needed her and might hold her in his arms so lovingly brought a new flush to her cheeks. Her eyes literally shone, and no one in the room could miss it.

On the drive home, Katie had remarked that, "Misty looks like a new person. Perhaps she really has found the one!"

Anything was possible.

In hindsight, it is amazing how little anyone at this end of the adventure knew about the person who had summoned these surprising and quite determined feelings from Misty. In hindsight, we were careless about the details, trusting Misty to have got most things right. As far as her mother and father were concerned, I think they didn't care if he was a chimpanzee. I was going, so nothing harmful would occur. Misty would have her adventure. She might learn some lessons, see a different country, and clear the dreams out of her head before starting work. That sounded pretty good to them. It might be that this young boy was all Misty thought him to be, in which case they would cross that bridge when they came to it. Who was to say, if his love for her was as strong as Misty thought, that he might not move over and join them in the village. Be the son they never had. At this stage, anything was possible. I'm probably getting carried away myself.

In hindsight, it is hard to imagine that a voyage of this magnitude would be made without more being known about the object of her adoration. It is strange that neither the father nor mother had asked to speak to the man who might become their son-in-law, but to some, it is understandable. More disasters, wrongs and crimes have been committed than can be measured because one person respects another's privacy. That was how it was with Misty and her parents. She had never been a cause for concern. Never sneaked out late at night to party with the village boys or indulged in periods of skipping school. Whatever her internal misgivings, she had always done the expected thing. This was the first time, in any major way, she had ever tried to set the agenda. Katie had been surprised by her determination, and her parents, David in particular, had grown increasingly concerned by events, but that was behind them now.

The air was cleared, the path was clear, and their little girl would be protected while she went out to meet her admirer. That night, as I lay in bed chewing over events and veering between exalted senses of my own nobility and a basic anguish and, dare I say it, lust, the Potts cuddled up in bed knowing their little family had faced uncharted waters but found a way through.

Margaret said to David, "If our Misty likes him, there is

much to like. We can be sure of that," and they both agreed.

The sad thing is that, taken from a certain perspective, in Bernard there was much to like. He was a decent man on many levels, who earned a living in a law abiding manner and had a talent for musical composition. On the face of it, a perfectly reasonable prospect as a son-in-law. The baldness might be a cause of laughter and some teasing, but that might be lived with. Ruby, even if she cared, would drift quietly into his unspoken history, but his two girls, and the fact that he was twenty years older than Misty, would take a lot of explaining, and the absence of a grandmother was a step beyond the ordinary. How he had managed to create so many falsehoods in the search of his dream was behind him. The secret was in his friend who didn't do dreams but only conquests.

At the same time as our crowd enjoyed a measure of sleep, in one form or another, Bernard could be found pacing round his room. The stillness of heart which he required to play the piano was nowhere to be found, and he was in some turmoil as events progressed. What is true is that, like Misty, he was enjoying the first unforced romance of his life. It might have come late in the day, but it was genuine for all that. He had to pray that somehow he would find a way through and have her in his life. To be loved was a natural desire, but to be understood so thoroughly as Misty did him was a prize he could not cast aside. Without any clear idea how it might be achieved, he prayed some solution made this new life possible.

~3~

It was the next day, in the next conversation, that Misty told Bernard the news. In earlier days, away from stress and plans, they had grown to call each other 'Blossom' and 'Tiger'. It was a ritual of innocence as they both revelled in the freedom to be themselves. In Bernard's case to be the person he wanted to be. The sillier and more childish they became, the more 'real' it all seemed. Free of stress, their love had grown and they had been able to make the other pretty much what they wanted in order to conduct the perfect love affair. With the news that Misty was actually coming over, and in two weeks, things took on a different tone. Naturally, the news that her cousin plus husband were also on the trip just added to the pressure.

As he heard the news, Bernard continued to smile, but now he felt the old game appearing. No longer able 'just to be himself' and be a sweet and gentle spirit who shared his music and his thoughts, he must pretend to be happier than he was. He was back there again, playing games and managing images. Through the fog of it, Misty was always gentle and beautiful, but he was very aware of the obstacles between his arms and her. He had no idea what her friends were like. Misty assured him that they were really nice. That Katie was her oldest friend and Bernard's greatest champion, and that I was a really solid man who would 'love you as soon as he sees you.' Bernard found that highly unlikely.

It is often sometime after you get the news that the full import of it begins to hit home. How he was to meet with Misty in the company of her friends, who were bound to be a bit watchful, and still drip feed the misunderstandings out in such a way as to minimise their impact? To begin with, he just got on with panicking. Pacing the floor, staring out of the window and watching television in that semi blind way that anxious people do.

After a time, he rang his friend Derek and said, as casually as possible, "Misty's coming over in two weeks, and she's bringing her cousin and her cousin's husband with her."

Derek was delighted. "Quite a party, then!"

For him, it was a simple case of 'game on or game over.' If it was game over just move on. One part of him was impressed that Bernard had actually persuaded some girl from half way round the world to come and see him – a pretty fair achievement, all in all – and the other half was relieved that things were coming to a head. To be honest, and that was something Derek did with reluctance, Bernie had become a bit of a drag recently. Mooning over the girl, and spending too much time going off on day dreams.

"Better come over, mate, let's talk it through," was his suggestion, and Bernard did just that. He was feeling out of his depth.

However generous of nature we are, we are all territorial about our friends. Derek was not all that generous, and would have been glad to hear the girl had vanished from the scene long ago but, in a way, this went one better. If they could 'reel her in' and have some fun that would be a feather in anyone's cap. Not easy if her friends were with her, but what was to lose? Derek's lack of emotion did Bernard some good. Of course, his friend missed the point. Despite all the falsehoods – and there were many – Bernard truly loved this girl, and as things now stood, she had been like a delicious flow of water through his arid emotional life, but he couldn't tell Derek that.

"Has she put on a show?" drew the answer, "No."

Again, Bernard tried not to be distressed by this simply manly question, and Derek was amazed that Bernard had missed a simple trick.

"Gotta have the pictures, mate," he reminded his friend. "Till they've got them out, you don't know where you are."

Again, Derek was on a different tack to his friend. It was hard to explain that it was precisely because he had not asked her 'to put on a show' or 'get them out' that Misty had grown to love him as she did. All talk of 'inner beauty' was lost on our cunning, worldly friend. He seldom stayed around long enough to get much sense of a girl's thoughts.

There is a story about him having loved a girl quite a few years ago, but he never referred to it. Very possibly, keeping his vulnerabilities under wraps was the safer course for him. The bare facts are that Derek did not do feeling. It was not worth the complications. He helped Bernard think of it more as a game, and being with his friend gave Bernard some perspective, but he was still infuriatingly particular about returning to his flat in time to have his daily chat. Whatever he might say to Derek, and sometimes to himself, that blessed tenderness had become an indispensable part of his life. He had the sense that his dream may not be forever, but he would cling to it while he could.

What if she really turned away? Then each day he had with her now would have to serve him for the rest of his life. He savoured every moment. Far from wanting to 'come clean' and clear up those little falsehoods which stood between him and true happiness, he became even more secretive. Now he was cruelly aware of passing time. Life without her was difficult to imagine.

Back home things were nicely in a whirl. Katie and Misty spent lots of time together, work permitting, as they planned the whole visit. Of course, the planning was largely Katie's, and she was doing everything she could to regain the control over her friend's romantic affairs. Like all skilful controllers, she moved carefully. To be honest, she hardly cared if the man in question was a tin of sardines. What stirred her was the shared adventure: the excitement, the travel, and the uncertainty. Having me along was a bit boring, but not unduly so.

She listened to Bernard's music without emotion before exclaiming, "That's so beautiful!"

Anything to show she was on board and one with her friend. Even Misty's mum and dad seemed less tense. They were concerned, of course, but they had no doubt, contrary to Katie's opinion, that I would keep a good handle on things, and keep them well informed. Not a spy, but just a protector in residence is how they saw me. My common sense and obvious affection were the guardians of their daughter.

During the week, as I sometimes did, I found myself up at the farm with David, and this time I had stopped by at the house to get the coffee.

"Ah, that's nice," he said seeing the mugs in my hand. He had no time for cups and never had. One brief look showed how he viewed me now. I had come up trumps, and put my own interests aside to look after his daughter.

"Take a good book. I would," he advised. "If you don't watch it, those two will chatter you to death on the plane," and we both smiled."

The simple telling of events seldom does them justice. Both Bernard and I, so different from each other, I liked to think, were hiding behind falsehoods. If David had got anywhere near my thoughts, he would have recoiled in horror, and if Misty knew the truth, how would she react? Both of us felt trapped by our circumstances. I had one advantage, if a slim one. All I had to do was wait it out. Not blow my cover. Act as the reliable and decent bore, and time would see me safely through to a more secure future. Who knows where Misty might end up, but at least I had a good chance of survival. The urgent, fussy, excitable attentions of my wife in all affairs made brooding that much harder. I found myself smiling at her antics.

Bernard was in a different situation. It would take great skill and candour to extricate himself from his situation. To tell her, as he honestly could, that – whatever the truth about his life and age and children – he truly loved her might save him. How many of us feel we can stand before a panel of our peers without artifice or deceit and still be admired. Not many, possibly, and Bernard had never been among that number. In him, Misty had found a man who would treasure her forever but who lacked the courage to be honest about himself. The absence of a sick grandmother was a problem on its own. He thought wildly of announcing that she had suddenly died, or moved to a home far away but never had the nerve to say either.

He sat, trapped by his own falsehoods and watched his future slide away. That brief time when he was at the centre of another's life. Oh, how he treasured the days when she talked with him and her tone was unguarded and free of doubt. He could not bear to sully her sweetness with the truth. He found it ironic that the most generous, tender, and caring emotions he had ever felt for another human being were hidden behind a barricade of falsehoods.

"I hate liars," she had once said, and of course he had agreed.

Everybody has to, but how many have not lied. Until Misty came into his life, he had never had the confidence to be himself and always sought disguise. Only in the darkness of the film theatre, the keyboard, or resting on Ruby's bed, had something like the real Bernard appeared.

He had allowed his friend to construct his profile, and now

he must live with the consequences. If he could not find courage, perhaps he could discover dignity. He dwelt upon this possibility. It is an irony of character that a man may exhibit both weakness and strength within a single breath. Yes, Bernard had lied, but he never tried to blame anyone else for his predicament. Whatever part Derek had played in the deception, Bernard never shied away from the truth when talking to himself. It was a quality in him that few would bother to notice.

Too soon, he feared, he would be back to a single life, but now the butt of some fresh ridicule. The object of his friend's merriment. He felt he had just moments to enjoy before the door closed on this precious chamber. With hindsight, he wished he'd been more honest from the start, but then, for him, it had all begun as a game, and he never dreamed of a connection like this.

Knowing what we know, it seems inconceivable that Misty was willing to travel so far with such a sketchy knowledge of her beau, but that was how it was. Something in Misty was summoned, and she seemed determined to celebrate it. Perhaps it was the sense of being independently in control of her life for the first time. Perhaps it was a feeling of shared frailties expressed through his music. I'm only guessing, but for the first time in her life, she was displaying a fearless determination to proceed. Everyone, from Katie through to her parents, baulked at warning her off her adventure. Her parents, certainly, had hoped from the beginning that the torch would flicker and go out, but they never made this opinion public. You know my position already, but I was not supposed to have an opinion. Katie, at face value also had no opinion but always craved excitement. Apart from cursory questions, no one from Misty through to her parents voiced concrete doubts. It was an accident of circumstances, a polite conspiracy to avoid the difficult question. It was the gap between our feelings and our speech. If things went wrong, the post-mortem would be ferocious, but for now, people just stood around in frozen uncertainty as events unfolded.

Everyone that is, but Misty.

Chapter Nine

As far as we in Misty's circle were concerned, here was another weightless moment. I've spoken of them before. David and Margaret, at least, felt they were facing their anxieties about Misty's romance. They knew I was going and that I would never let anything bad happen to her. To them, and probably Misty, I presumed, I was somewhere between a caring big brother and a cousin. I was family at least, and a trusted member of the clan. My presence made the difference. The only fly in the ointment was that my feelings were not as they supposed. A greater compliment had never been paid to me in my entire life, and my feelings had never been so misunderstood.

I have spoken before, and know about the beauty of self-sacrifice. Of those who put the greater good before self-interest. Oh, how we love to read those stories of some man or women whose deeds, unrecognised at the time, speak of a sense of honour few lay claim to. In my time, I had done one or two minor acts which might be characterised in this way. I will not bore you with the details, but the 'afterglow' was beautiful in itself. The feeling of being part of some angelic symphony, the music behind life which shows man his inner greatness: selfless, modest, brave.

Am I getting carried away? Very possibly, but these self-debates were among the things which had kept my spirit afloat when life seemed unjust, or just unbearable.

Katie was full of the adventure. Being part of this great saga, as she thought it, was wonderful in itself, but add the romance of a long trip to a new country and continent, and we are moving her towards a glimpse of paradise. I have always thought that to be truly happy a man must be a part of something larger than himself and be aware of it. It might be faith, or the changing seasons. The movement of the tides, a noble war, or self-sacrifice. The list is pretty endless, but whatever it was, Katie felt it at this moment, and it made her sunnier than I had ever seen her. I was canny enough to 'catch the wave,' and made I sure I said nothing which would dampen the mood.

"I'm sure this guy is everything you would expect. Misty knows what's valuable in life," and other statements to show I was as swept up in the adventure as her.

It was my opinion at the time that Misty had only an untested idea about what was valuable in life, and I could see from Katie's eyes that she felt the same way. Possibly we were underestimating Misty. The heart of her charm was her innocence. No one knew of her experiences in college. This was not the time to cloud our anticipation by a fixation with the small print. We could worry about that later. Both of us, in our own vague and misguided way, believed that if we were part of the trip, nothing could go seriously wrong. Don't you love the ways we all deceive ourselves?

In Perth, Derek was already gaining some currency from the event. He could see that Bernard was writhing for some mysterious reason. Those who believed that honour meant more than strategies were deluding themselves, as far as Derek was concerned, and usually provided him with easy pickings. Bernard was his only exception, but he was still surprised by the way a few 'marketing gambits' might cause his friend sleepless nights. In Derek's eyes, all you needed to love was in the mirror, and to leave yourself hostage to the feelings of another was to expose yourself to harm from forces beyond control.

I suspect there was more to it than that, but the experience or trauma, if any, which led him to this barren point of view is not known to me. I comfort myself that people of this type wake up one day and the full force of awareness falls upon them. They are paralysed with regret about their acts of cruelty and die in a state of agony and contrition. Another side of me thinks all that is rubbish, and it is like asking a crocodile to feel compassion for the duck it eats while leaving the ducklings as orphans. To the crocodile the ducklings are merely the next meal, deliciously unprotected, but to me, they are an image of hand-wringing agony and sadness. Some people share our planet but not our values. Derek, to me, was one of those.

Possibly, he helped to keep poor Bernard 'grounded' with his 'plenty more fish in the sea' approach to dating. Certainly, in his company, Bernard affected some bravado. He didn't want to be exposed as one of those wimpy romantic gargoyles who are the laughingstock of every bar. He kept his secret values to himself, though some traces of them effected the way he spoke. The truth is that he had now adopted the posture of a death row inmate, and pessimism filled his thoughts.

He could not imagine how it would be that a girl as delicate as Misty would accept his 'marketing' falsehoods and reach out to the gentle being within. Anything was possible, he prayed. The thought of losing her was unbearable. Who knows what last minute reprieve might be granted. Possibly, her love of him and admiration for his talents was larger than he supposed. Possible was all he had. He had no way of knowing at this stage.

We were flying out on the Thursday, so to mark the event, the whole 'immediate' family gathered for a meal at Katie's mum and dad's. Mrs Ballard, as I called her, thought herself a gifted chef and had the ability to surprise guests on occasion. More often, she did not. In the main, her food was passable, though ornately displayed on a table laid with care. I was always full of wonder that a meal for close family might include carefully folded napkins, and other signs of social finery. Certainly, neither David nor Margaret could care less about such things, and nor could I or Geoff, but Katie and her mother had their standards. Nothing was more important, day to day, than appearances, and after all, this was a special meal.

Daring to take the lead, and determined to show I was

'onside' with Katie and Misty, I raised my glass to toast 'the happy couple.' I think everyone had left reality at the door, and just talked positively about a situation they barely understood. I've done that before, but usually when the outcome is of no consequence to me. Now the plot was more important than I could admit.

Misty, full of love and excitement, seemed especially intoxicating to me, and then she turned to me with a compelling softness and inclusion, as though we had a pact, and said, "Here's to Bill, whose doing more than anyone could ask to make me happy."

As her soft, knowing, and beguiling gaze flowed over my defences I was only dimly aware of the other's saying, "Here, here," and, "Good old Bill."

I think they took my look of lost confusion to be modesty and found that most appealing. In some ways, I was like the hero of the hour, but I felt more like the secret betrayer. There was something in her eyes which had more knowledge than I liked, which seemed to peer inside my desires and see her picture there. That she was an object of worship in my sad and deceitful life. Without knowing it, I was tasting the same fruit as Bernard at the very moment I was being feted.

I made a point, for the rest of the evening, of acting as though I had little involvement in the matter. As if it was a small thing to ask and could hardly be called a favour. That Misty was of no personal importance to me other than as the daughter and companion of my wife and friends. More than anything, I tried to display this sense to Misty, but I had some horrible sense that, like that girl at the café, she had seen inside my soul and knew an aspect of me no one else would recognise.

I kept my eyes firmly on her face if I addressed her, although this took a conscious act of will. I made a point of showing everyone the same level of attention and placing my arm affectionately round my wife's shoulders in a carefully random act of affection. Katie, certainly, seemed warmed by this, and both sets of parents behaved as if I was 'one of the good ones.' Despite all this, I could not shake off the horrid sense that Misty had picked up on my true emotions. When she looked at me, part of me was swooning, but the more conscious part suspected that she was toying with me, playing with me, and she knew that, once in Australia, she would get me to approve her choice whatever my own opinions. I felt ill.

Thus, I left the Ballard house quite late in the evening. Feted as a hero and admired by all but one: the person I most loved. I had never felt so exposed and swore to myself that I would do anything to prove to Misty that she had mistaken my feelings. That I really was as boring and detached as others believed.

That night, Katie did something unusual. She did not invoke the unwritten 'no touch' rule but pressed herself against me till even Mr. Plod, my secret name for my erotic awareness, understood that action was required. There seemed a new born passion in her, a new freshness, as though she was rediscovering me all over again. Her own, sweet Bill, her Mr. Dependable whose support was always patient and without limit. I still do not really know what to think, but when she looked at me, her eyes almost glowed, and I could hardly understand these new emotions. In every way, the evening had been disorientating, and I was at a loss at how to feel.

Our passion spent, she did not turn away, but laid her head upon my shoulder and seemed more open and vulnerable to me than I could ever remember. What was going on? I could hardly make sense of it. Cheered by all, but known by just one. Even as I lost myself in pleasure, those eyes of Misty's played with my mind and left me fearing for my reputation. Had I been unmasked by the last person I needed to know my secret? As Katie clung to me, I now clung to her. At some subconscious level, I felt my circumstances were threatened, and I was in danger of losing everything I valued. I swore to myself that I would exercise greater control. Misty, possibly, was more dangerous than I realised, and proving her mistaken was now a priority.

It was nice to have Katie show me this new 'regard,' but the 'Misty episode'… Was I mistaken? Guilt may have exaggerated her look in my eyes. My mind went round and round and found no peace on its journey. I was resolved to watch my behaviour.

Nothing is more frightening to a man with secrets than an observant woman, and my sweet, delicate, and impressionable Misty had shown a side of her which I had never suspected. I had forgotten that she had been blessed with looks well above average, and those looks gain you the attention others work harder to attract. Misty was used to both attracting and ignoring attention. That young, cheery boy at the sweet corn party was not an uncommon occurrence, and she normally dealt with all admirers in the same way.

How stupid of me to believe that my secretive, disloyal and furtive admirations would pass unknown to a girl used to scenting the slightest wisp of admiration. What I had not taken into account is that she might both notice it and say nothing to her friends. There was a level of the discrete in Misty which went unrecognised. To us she was just 'the sweet one.' No one bothered to look more deeply at her character.

Certainly, in the way Katie and the parents had reacted, they all took me at face value. The trip took on a new and challenging profile. I would have to show powers of detachment beyond anything I had had ever shown if I was to persuade Misty that she had been mistaken. As sleep overcame me, I promised myself that I would make that happen. That David and Margaret would be right to trust me. That Misty would not look at me again.

But still the thought persisted. That for all my careful behaviour, she had seen through my front of slightly unintelligent and long suffering devotion to my wife, and my scrupulous and detached management of her father's business affairs. She sensed some soft, seedy underbelly, where my hunger for her body and her love dwelt on my desires.

In more ways than I feared, she had me in her pocket, and she knew it. Whatever she wanted to do with Bernard, she knew I would not have the nerve to say anything about it. That I was a man prey to his own devious appetites and recognised as one by the object of his fantasies. That I would not have the courage to do the very thing I was being entrusted to do. That I was a coward prey to his own devious appetites.

I could go on and on. I am going on and on. Peering over

the abyss robbed my senses of all proportion.

~2~

With much in your life you rely on everything to stay unchanged so you can do as you like. We do it unconsciously. It's a presumption we use in order to make life manageable. Now, as I lay in bed awake long after the sleeping hour, I began to wonder if my image of sweet Misty might not be missing a couple of vital aspects. There was a knowing amusement in her glance at me over dinner, which was far from the girl who inspired the protective in all who meet her. Suddenly, I wished I was not going on the trip. I was getting out of my depth, and relying on someone not to push the buttons which should not be pushed.

In the morning, pretending to be refreshed, I got up and made the tea as usual. Neither of us was at work today, and I was just organising some papers while Katie got on with the packing, an exercise which seemed to involve endless discussions over which dresses to be taken. It was a process which usually amused me, but not today. Now I was filled with nothing but anxiety. I seemed to have a premonition that my current circumstances were threatened.

Katie was in one of those rare moods when the sun shined out of every crack in the universe. I was downstairs clearing up some paperwork while she moved around upstairs organising clothes and bags.

"How many shirts?" and other questions filtered down the stairs.

As I bent over my desk, I heard a crashing sound followed by screaming. I rushed into the hall, and there was Katie in a heap at the bottom of the stairs and with the calf of her right leg going off at a strange angle. It was clearly broken.

I become detached at such moments, and moved without comment to phone for an ambulance. They said they would be here in ten minutes, and to leave the phone lines open. I then bent over Katie, who was somewhere between screaming and crying. I was prompted to ask what happened but decided not to. Clearly, she had fallen down the stairs and broken her leg. Why she had fallen down was not important at the moment. I peered up the stairs to see if I could spot something obvious, but there was nothing. For now, I was just concerned with the practical details. Later, I would reflect on the implications.

Sure enough, the ambulance turned up a mere five minutes late, and keeping Katie near calm in that period was no easy thing. They gave her an injection to help with the pain and set about getting her on the stretcher. I rang her mum and dad and we agreed to meet up at the hospital.

Soon, everyone was there, at a gathering without joy. Katie's dad was composed, as you might expect, and her Mum was tearful and anxious. She had broken her leg but, luckily, no other injury had been suffered. It could have been worse. She was in the operating theatre having her leg set while we all milled around outside. Nothing was said about the trip. I caught Misty's eye once, by mistake, but she seemed distracted and far from the girl who had unsettled me on the previous day. At last, Katie appeared on a trolley and was wheeled off to a bed.

"How are you feeling, darling," and other nonsense were spoken over her drowsy head, but she appeared to be unaware of her environment.

As the dust settled on the horrible accident, the topic of Misty's visit to Australia was raised by her father.

"Well I suppose that puts the kybosh on the Australia trip." he said tactfully.

Misty looked straight at him, calm but single minded and said, "Look, Dad, I'm gutted about Katie, but I'm still going. It was your idea she came, but it won't stop me if she can't."

Such a conversation had never been heard in the Potts family, and you could sense the shock in the room.

Margaret looked at her daughter and said in that calm voice of hers, "Let's not be rude Misty," but Misty promptly left the room, her face crumpling as she did so.

David looked around him and said, "We'd better go after her," and off they went, leaving me with Katie's parents. My interests had left the room, but my responsibilities remained within it.

I shook my head as boring people do, and turned my attention towards Katie, because that is what faithful people do. As I leaned forward and brushed her hair away from her eyes in a gesture of concern, I let my mind wander up the hill to where the Potts family must be having their inaugural argument. I cannot swear that they had never had a disagreement, but they always acted as if they didn't, and I'd never witnessed one. I continued sitting by the bed in a display of unquestioning devotion until Katie's mother and father left to go to bed.

As he left, Geoff laid his hand on my shoulder and said, "Look after her, lad" in the way which confirmed I already was doing so.

Katie seemed drowsy but not in pain. She kept looking at her caste, and I asked her if she wanted me to sign it. There was no humour in her eyes or forbearance or any of those stoic qualities which people so enjoy.

"You should have been helping, then this never would have happened."

The remark was typical of her, and I just shook my head. What was the point of arguing now? There was no real energy in her anyway. She railed against the fates and me, their representative, until sleep overtook her. The nurse came in at last, and suggested that I might go home, "She's in safe hands," and that kind of thing.

I rose with apparent reluctance, and to be honest, to see her sitting there all trapped and robbed of purpose disturbed me more than it should. As if this freak accident might open the portal to a new and uncertain future.

Katie had courage and determination and standards. She was not silly in her manner when at work. Being silly and displaying minor tantrums was just her way of unwinding, and I had known her long enough to understand this. Her complaining at me was just another sign of her unhappiness at her new immobility. Not to be going to Australia was one thing, but to be stuck in this way, at the mercy of my clumsy quality of care was quite another.

After I left, I went up to her mum and dad's to discuss the situation, and Mrs Ballard said, "It might be better if you both come and stay here for a bit while she settles down. You don't want to be tied down with nursing her, and I'd enjoy the company."

It was a kindness, and I agreed. At that moment, I would have agreed to anything. All I wanted was my bed to which I now retreated. As always when you find yourself suddenly alone, the place seemed unnaturally empty. I found myself missing her, and it struck me how much I did. That old saying about not missing people till they're gone came to mind. With silence as my companion, I experienced a rare feeling of emptiness, an echo of my life before I had met Katie.

You may not have gathered it from me before, but in many ways Katie had saved me. Until I met her, I had spent too long watching life and not enough time living it. The reason I kept metaphorically walking into things was because I was always fascinated by what was around me. Katie was both a dreamer and a snatcher of trinkets. She could be profound and facile in alternate breaths. It was a hard profile to live with. I suppose, like a shark, she had to keep swimming, hunting, and chasing, but in those rare moments when she allowed herself to glide through life, she could be surprisingly reflective and almost admit that the hurried part of her was a diversion or disguise. At heart, she understood what was significant. At these times she reminded me of her dad, but as I lay there alone in our bed, I thought of those moments when she turned to me, and knowledge was in her eyes. That is when I remembered why I loved her and realised I still did.

I was boring now, but I had not always been so. At college, after leaving my father's austere regime, I had discovered the benefits of drinking and company and girls and found myself revelling in all three. Not that successfully, mind you. I don't want to give a greater impression of my abilities than is accurate, but I had some success purely through effort.

The 'meeting' of Katie and I was unusual for a future husband and wife. I was walking back to my flat when I saw a girl crouched over in a doorway being ill. Why she was on her own I did not know, but I did not feel I could leave her there. When I asked her if she was alright, she stared at me as though I was from outer space.

"Where do you live?" and, "Are you alright?" both met with no response.

In the end I felt I had no alternative but to guide her back to my flat, which I did. She came without protest. In these circumstances I was always the gentleman. Well, to be honest, nothing like this had ever happened to me, but I think I would always have been protective faced with a situation like this. I helped her up the stairs, and laid her on the bed fully clothed and placed a blanket over her, and a washing up bowl by her side, in case things went from bad to worse.

In the morning, when I popped my head round the door, to see if she wanted tea or water or breakfast she was sitting up and looking confused.

"I don't know if you remember, but you were a bit ill last night, and lost, so I brought you back here."

I could see from her expression that she was initially suspicious, but then she realised she was still dressed and safe, and possibly I was not a villain or a criminal. I offered her a bathrobe and asked her if she wanted a bath or a shower. Leaving her to clean herself up, I went off to prepare some toast and tea and waited for her in the living room.

Impressively, she had cleaned up pretty well and did not complain of feeling too ill. I pretended not to notice too much, but she was a striking and pretty girl of about 5ft 8inches with longish naturally curly black hair. She had a nice, slim figure with just the right amount of curves, but her manner was crestfallen and introverted. I made a point of remaining warm but professional. Anyone would have been struck by her looks, but I felt this was not the time to notice them. Later, she said that was one of the things which most impressed her.

It turned out she had had some dreadful row with her

boyfriend and had run off into the night so that he wouldn't find her. He was quite a new connection, apparently, and it also appeared she was not his only girlfriend. That had come to light earlier in the evening when some other girl, who he thought was out of town, walked up to their table in the restaurant, grabbed his glass of wine and emptied it over his head.

Before storming off, the girl had turned to Katie and said, "He's a bastard. He'll only make you cry."

Of course, an argument followed, during which, almost without noticing, she had drained most of the wine bottle down her throat. They left the table, and once outside, things got pretty heated. She is not sure what happened: whether she ran off, or he stalked off. Either way, when I found her, she was on her own.

It then transpired that she was one of those impetuous people who act first and collect their wits later. She had already moved in with him, after only a month of knowing him, and now had nowhere else to stay. You've guessed it. I said she could park herself with me while she sorted herself out, and the rest, as they say, is history.

Well, not quite history. I, myself, was in a bit of a bind. I had been working for a small business as a book keeper and managed to start an affair with the wife of the boss while accepting his wages. It had all been exciting and dramatic, and both his wife and I had loved the adventure and secrecy of it until he found out. I'm not sure what happened to her, but I was sacked, of course. Apparently, we were seen by someone in the town, and he had us followed by some private eye. I don't think he was too concerned with me, whom he described as 'scum' in one of our short later conversations, but they had two small children, and I think he was trying to get the evidence to obtain custody of them when they became divorced.

It is a strange anomaly of character that a man who can be selfish and wanton in one scenario can also act with honour in another. That is not accepted wisdom, but I have found it to be true. For myself, faced with a 'damsel in distress,' I would try and act in accordance with the highest standards, almost as if I was in a play. Thus it was with Katie that I, who had just been chucked out of a job by a husband I had cuckolded, now acted in the slightly stiff and correct manner that only an inhibited man of honour would employ. At least I thought so.

I won't bother to go into it too much, but for me, being in society was very much like being in a play. My father believed in performance more than anything else.

I remember him saying to me, "No one is interested in whether you are happy or sad, boy. They are interested in whether you are here or not, and your work is of a sufficient standard to complete the job. Never forget that."

Doing the job well, and 'fitting in' became what I was good at. My Achilles tendon was getting bored and a lack of intimacy – a condition more prevalent than I realised. I used to feel a weariness come over me in some social circle, relationship, or occupation, and then everything would fall apart. Luck had rescued me more than once.

Now I had found a place where I was renewed and welcomed. Where my happiness seemed to matter, and I resolved not to threaten that in any way. I would become the man I had been playing.

Chapter Ten

Sometime later, when I had risen and was about to go up to the Ballard house to see Katie and her Mum and Dad, the phone rang, and it was David Potts on the line.

"Morning, Bill, hope you slept as well as expected. I've been speaking to Sandra, Geoff, and Katie, and they've agreed with me that it would be OK for you to go to Australia with Misty, as long as you're happy to do so. I'm just not happy about her going on her own."

Needless to say, my voice was much calmer than my emotions, but I had some trouble controlling it.

"What's Misty say about it?" I asked.

"Oh, she's more than happy," said David. "She thinks you will be great company."

"Well, I'm off up to Katie's now," I replied. "So I'll give you a reply from there."

After I had finished the call, I felt like having a swift whisky or six, but it was only eight thirty in the morning. I made myself a tea and sat down. My published position was that I had a brotherly and protective view of Misty. In fact, I was sure, at this stage, that I could still keep my real feelings under wraps and delight in the feeling of medieval self-sacrifice that produced, unless those emotions were fanned by the lady herself. I saw no reason why that might happen.

Until the weekend, I had been confident that Misty, herself, had no awareness of my feelings, and I had deluded myself into believing I presented a warm but enigmatic exterior. Throughout my marriage and time in the village, I had been sure to present the very picture of correctness, but that brief but knowing look she gave me had unsettled me. I did not dare investigate it further, and I was comforted by the fact that the whole trip was built on her love for another man. I was confident that as long as I stayed warm but impersonal, and listened with approval to her gushing over Bernard, all might still be well. Whatever his qualities, he stood between me and social and emotional chaos, so he had my unquestioning support. I was sure that a girl of Misty's qualities would not give her heart lightly, and anyone worthy of her respect automatically had mine. I made a promise to myself not to drink too much in her company. In my experience, when people are drunk, they never lie but are often rash about what they reveal. Clarity of mind was what I needed now.

Don't you love the way you sometimes look back at things and realise how pompous your thought processes can be? I was suffering from that dangerous delusion people suffer from when they believe their own marketing materials. There were some grounds for optimism. Misty had certainly given me 'the look,' but it had been backed by amusement rather than agenda. As long as I stayed calm and took some books with me, all might be well.

When I arrived at the Ballard house, I was met by Katie's mum, who smiled at me as though I had already 'saved the day.' I had a horrid feeling I was being cast as the hero of the hour, and never has a role been less deserved. Needs must, and I smiled with selfless forbearance as the burdens of my responsibility were outlined to me.

They heaped praise on my unworthy shoulders, and I shrugged and said, "What must be must be," and any other platitude which came to mind.

Gradually the shock of it was subsiding, and I was now warming to the new profile. I continued to remind myself that

Misty's eyes were truly focused on Bernard, and any looks she cast in my direction were just for entertainment. There was no agenda in them, I was sure of that.

Comforted by that thought, which I repeated obsessively to myself, I went upstairs to see to Katie. As I entered her room, she was sitting up in bed and smiled at me warmly.

"How's the hero of the hour?" she asked, and before I could reply she added, "Poor you. I don't know anyone less interested in travel or romance."

"What must be must be," I replied – it seemed to be my phrase of the moment – and then bent to give her a kiss. She is, as you may have gathered, a capricious woman, but when you are in her good books, the sun shines on you, and no favour is too great to grant. I realised that Katie had been worried that 'the great adventure' would fail at the first hurdle if she was not able to go. She'd heard what Misty said, but I don't think she gave it too much weight. She seemed unusually selfless about things, but she certainly was very disappointed not to be going and to witness the last reel of the 'the great romance.'

After a short period of gushing, she got on with the business of warning me against 'putting a spanner in the works.'

"I know you feel very protective about Misty, but she loves this man. Don't start getting all big brotherly with her. She's old enough to look after herself. It's only Uncle David who's insisting on you going. It doesn't mean anything."

The inference was that, while her place on the trip was critical, mine was just as a fill-in. As I knew myself, her views were in direct opposition to Misty's parents, but I didn't feel like pointing that out. If I hadn't been so nervous of my own feelings I might have laughed then, because no one was less able than Katie to allow others to 'follow their own destiny' unless she's had a pretty big hand in shaping it.

Observing lack of self-awareness in others was one of my hobbies, and it helped me take the pressure off myself. I let her ramble on as she warmed to her theme, and she was then joined by her mother carrying a tray of tea and toast. She was happy to chime in with her daughter, and both exhorted the well-meaning emotional dullard, namely me, not to be shy about lending Misty support in any decision she might make. That Misty might be wrong, or in any danger, or liable to make a fool of herself, or anything other than be on the first steps to romantic paradise never entered the conversation. Geoff, whose head I had always thought more ordered on these subjects had found something important to do in the garden and was keeping well out of the way. Perhaps he thought David and Sandra might speak the words he would have spoken. I've no idea.

Having finished my breakfast, I prepared to go and see the Potts family, with Katie saying as a last rejoinder, "I've no idea how he is going to be able to finish the packing on his own," which made her mother laugh and me shrug my shoulders, everything you'd expect at such a time.

When I got to the Potts house, they all gathered round me in the hall. Misty was staring at me, but her eyes shone without agenda. They'd faced their first crisis as a family and found the solution, namely me. Everywhere I went, it seemed, I was the hero of the hour. I was ready to go through to the living room when David asked me if I would like to have a quick look at some new plants he had got. Everyone knew he wanted to chat with me on my own, but no one objected.

Sure enough, as soon as we got inside the greenhouse he started off, without even pretending to point out any new species. "You'll be told a lot of nonsense I know" he said, "but just remember, you are there to keep your eye on Misty. Ring me as much as you like, and don't worry about the time. I love the girl, but she can be impulsive, and she and Katie together are a nightmare."

I nodded my agreement and prepared to speak but he just continued.

"At the first sign of trouble, or if you think the guy's a nutter, just stand up to him. I'm relying on you to look after Misty, and I know you'll do me proud, but don't be swayed by her tears if anything goes wrong."

There was always a problem with David when he was being very serious because his clothing was often on the odd side, but now he was so focused and intent that I paid no attention to his wardrobe. All signs of eccentricity seemed to have disappeared, and I was faced with a man protecting his family. It was clear that he had absolute faith in my loyalty and commitment to the cause, even if he was worried about my willpower when faced by female cunning. If he knew my true feelings, I can hardly imagine what his emotions would have been.

I kept asking myself what my 'true feelings' were. They seemed to change by the hour and the company, but my thoughts about Misty were certainly growing stronger and more persistent. I am too shy to go on about her physical attributes, but I've said before she was above averagely attractive. In fact, I have to say that, for a girl with such a pure reputation, she had an undercurrent of sexual awareness and magnetism. I am not objective on the subject and even now feel uncomfortable talking about it, but that knowing look and the sense of her confidence in her dealings with me was more than unsettling. Do you see how I become the man I wish to be in my speech patterns. It would be humorous if it was not tragic.

I thanked the powers that be once again that I was not the object of her affections. Before me stood her father still talking to me with words which had trouble drowning out my daydreams, a man I admired more than any other for the way he had built a life and family of such strength and independence in a world I found it difficult to navigate. Even Katie, who could irritate me to the point of madness, seemed more precious as our union was threatened by my travels. I felt like a man looking at a delicious meal through a locked glass door. Should someone unlock that door I knew resistance would be very hard.

We had one full day left before we left for the airport so, for me, more than time enough to finish packing. We were leaving at some ridiculous hour in the morning to get to the airport for the flight which was at seven-thirty. The whole journey lasted over a day plus checking in and getting through customs at the other end. We were flying from Exeter via Singapore. Neither of us had been on any journey close to this in our lives. I never liked travelling at the best of times. Hours of mindless hanging around and then being at the mercy of whoever was transporting you, but there was nothing to do but grin and bear it. Stoicism was meant to be one of my main values, and I knew I would need all the patience I could summon.

Misty herself seemed silent. She rarely spoke directly to me, and it seemed strange that we would be spending all this time together. My obsession with her was private and largely by means of my imagination and her manner of speaking with you. The irony was, in real life terms, we were barely more than strangers. I felt there were plenty of reasons to be nervous.

~2~

It had been decided that we would all convene for the final meal before our journey at Geoff and Mrs. Ballard's house, as I persisted in thinking of her, which we duly did. Katie was transported down to the living room and we sat around her 'enjoying' a sort of picnic. David was driving us to the airport, and I could see he was edgy. He kept shooting me 'You'll do fine' glances, but I thought he was trying to comfort himself more than me. Geoff kept well out of it, apart from offering drinks and being unusually helpful with the plates. Misty wanted to have one last chat with Bernard in private, so we were on our own briefly.

More directly, David said to me, "Just bring her back safe," and I can say I had never seen him so edgy and unsure, this man of daily vision and remoteness from everyday anxieties.

What we could not see and did not know, was that as Bernard sat down to chat with Misty, he felt about as nervous as her dad but for different reasons. He, himself, felt swept along by events and not in control of them. Derek clearly thought the whole thing was a laugh and was not being much in the way of an emotional support. He did his best to control himself, but his sweetheart, always so attuned to his moods and fears moved to reassure him.

"There's nothing to worry about, darling," the word came

naturally to her now. "I know who you are, and once we hold each other, everything else will be fine. Don't worry about Bill. He'll do whatever I want. He won't interfere."

To those of us who knew her in what we might call her daily life, this assertiveness and sense of control would have been astonishing. Clearly, she had come a long way from that shy and pliable girl we downstairs still thought she was.

Although she could not see him, and that always irritated her, he sent her new photos on request but had never got the camera thing sorted, she always managed to quieten him with her words, and once again, he dared to dream that somehow, when she came, the magic would persist, and his life would be forever changed. His mood lasted as long as the call, but as she said her last goodbye and spoke the last words she would via the internet, his anxieties moved back from the shadows and engulfed him. How had he become so vulnerable? Perhaps a drink might help?

Back in the living room, David suggested they all call it an early night. It just felt strange to me. The girl I hungered for but with whom I barely conversed and I were setting off on this journey together. The sense that we were sharing something, however ill-defined it might be, was present in our eyes as we said goodnight. Her gaze was friendly but also controlled.

Both Katie and her mum seemed sad, and I gave them a good hug before I left. With Katie, there was a sense of sadness and regret. Mad as it sounded, on some levels, I wished she was coming with us. Then our adventure would be difficult but nothing like the ordeal and examination it now threatened to be. The plan was that I would meet them there early, and David, Misty, and I would set off in his car. As things got nearer, they seemed harder to process. Sleep was not going to come easily.

In Australia, in a mood which mirrored mine in many ways, Bernard could be found pacing up and down anxiously wondering how he was going to be able to orchestrate his initial meeting with Misty. Couples normally have problems when a big lie is exposed at any time in a relationship, but on the first physical meeting, the pressures seemed almost beyond endurance. Add the distance and the travelling, and the situation was outside anything he could imagine. What had he been thinking? He felt stupid and desperate. If only he didn't love her so much he might relax, but however much he lied about his circumstances, he knew his feelings were real. It was the honesty of them which had drawn her to him in the first place. The irony was not lost on him. He kept playing over different scenarios in his head but none of them seemed to give him much hope.

"There are a couple of misunderstandings I want to clear up," seemed a bit lame, and, "My sick grandmother doesn't exist," a bit harsh, as did all the other openings which came to mind.

This girl who listened to his musical outpourings with wonder, and treated all his anxieties with tenderness and understanding had been like a miracle in his life, and he had become more open on more levels with her than with anyone in his life before. That all this was sullied by lies and misdirection encouraged by Derek's cheerful and irresponsible influence did not make them easier to live with. He wracked his brains for some way out but saw, increasingly, that he would just have to throw himself on her mercy and beg for understanding. Possibly not the best way to impress a lady when you first meet her.

He longed for that elusive calm and clarity, but at the moment, he seemed to be descending into a deeper, blacker panic. He felt almost nauseous, and his skin felt clammy. As he paced, he was aware that only hours separated him from the meeting. In a wild train of thought, he considered not turning up at the airport at all, and just leaving his absence to give her the message, but he could not bring himself to do it. There are few moments in life when we are confronted unambiguously with the consequences of an error. More often than not, some twist of good fortune or circumstance intervenes to soften the blow. Why it was that one of the most timid of men should be left alone to deal with the full implication of his deceit is a question I still ask myself. Even now, I feel a sympathy for Bernard, whose weaknesses seem a curious mirror of my own.

It is a fact of life that many friendships are based on the capacity for one friend and his chaos to entertain another without prompting too much sympathy. In this case, the deeper Bernard got into the mire, the more it seemed to amuse Derek, who still considered the impending arrival of Misty to be a form of entertainment. For a man who hardly understood the word commitment and who would not admit to any vulnerability except for marketing purposes, seeing Bernard writhing at the prospect of his imminent exposure was not far short of hilarious. He kept that too himself. He dimly understood that, for Bernard, there were not 'plenty more fish in the sea,' but that is as far as it went. It was with some difficulty that Bernard persuaded him that his presence at the airport might be unhelpful, but he looked forward to hearing about it later in the day. Essentially, for Bernard, there was nothing to do but wait, but waiting can be the hardest task of all. He struggled with each hour and almost exhausted the hands of his watch by continuously checking them.

In the air, we sat pleasantly side by side, filling the time with sleep and occasional comments about the flight. Misty, to me, seemed full of a suppressed excitement, but she was not going to start gushing in my ear about her love for this other man. How much she understood my thoughts and feelings for her, many of them far from pure, I had no real clue at this stage, but I lived in fear of her perceptions. I was reading a book on the history of the German imperial family for no reason at all, apart from the fact that it was interesting and might provide greater cover for myself as Mr. Boring and a possible subject for neutral conversation.

Yes, that is how I thought. It was a bit like trying to build tank traps out of matchsticks, but I could think of little else. Her proximity and the occasional warmth of her arms as they touched disturbed me, and when I say I read the book, I more truthfully stared at its pages as my mind dwelt on the person beside me. The flight droned on and on and some films were available to pass the time, but mainly I tried to read or sleep while remaining friendly but unengaged.

~3~

Unlike me, Misty was enjoying the flight. She had never been on a plane before and everything that happened was a first and an adventure. She was no fool and had been aware that Bernard was uneasy, the silly boy. His vulnerability made her smile, but she was always sure she could settle any nerves he felt when they met. Her ability to calm him and the sense of control it gave her was one of the things she enjoyed most. Apart from a few pets, she had never had such influence on anyone else. And then there was his talent. She had not shared it much, apart from a few snatches of a song with Katie, but the way he sang and wrote lyrics moved her more than she could say. That quality of expressing desire and isolation mirrored much of her own experience.

Sometimes, as I sat beside her studying my book with unusual concentration, she made a point of brushing my arm with hers just to feel the slight squirm she got when she did it. My infatuation with her, which she had noticed over time had remained unannounced. Who would she talk about it to without creating a giant fuss, and she hated fuss, but my feelings amused her.

She was certain I would never try anything with her, and that was a large part of the charm of the situation, but she enjoyed toying with me just a little bit. With Katie out of the way, she promised herself that she would tease me just a bit more to pass the time. All at once, she felt liberated and adventurous after a lifetime fenced within others' expectations. Even in the cramped conditions of the plane, her new sense of freedom was exhilarating. She was more sure of Bernard than she had been of anyone in her life, and his desperate nervousness made her all the more anxious to be by his side and protect him.

The thought of being introduced to his friends, and meeting his grandmother of whom he spoke so fondly kept her thoughts warm as she sneaked the odd look at his photo on her mobile. She knew it was meant to be off, but who would ring her up here, and what harm could it do? For fun, she stretched out and brushed my leg by mistake. My face was a picture to her. She felt both faithful and mischievous as hell. This was going to be her life changing adventure, and nothing was going to stop her enjoying it to the full.

She loved her mum and dad more than anyone could

imagine, but their world suddenly seemed so small to her as she jetted across the world. How well she knew that if they or even Katie had been with her she could not have got anywhere near having so much fun but with 'Mr. Putty' beside her. She was free to do as she liked and knew I would not prevent her. Bring it on. The adventure of a lifetime. When she first started her internet dating experience who would have thought she would find a man so special, or be here with Mr. Putty somewhere over the Pacific Ocean on the way to her first real adventure.

Those ghosts from her college days seemed to have vanished from her thoughts in these new surroundings. Being with me made her feel safe and yet free. It was an entirely new experience, and she was going to drain it to the last drop. As I sat beside her, thankfully unaware of most of her daydreams, she kept smiling to herself and listening to some music through her earphones. She seemed free from fatigue and more alive than I had ever seen her before. Sometimes she would touch me as she moved slightly to the music, and once her foot brushed mine. The electric shock that went through me at this unexpected intimacy was hidden, I hoped, from this girl lost in her thoughts and music.

Despite the length of the journey, both of us seemed surprisingly free of fatigue. She because of her new adventure and sense of liberation, and I because I felt horribly alert and uneasy. I did my best to keep my mind off events by thinking of poor Katie stuck in bed with her broken leg. Let's be honest, the thought of any difficulty she might be going through seemed small compared to mine, but I did my best to keep only normal thoughts passing through my mind. Once, Misty leaned over and asked me how the book was going. I realised I had not turned over a page for some time, so I told her it was, "a bit boring, really," and tried to smile but felt faintly transfixed by a look of amusement I saw behind her eyes and that strange knowingness which was becoming more and more unsettling.

How I was to get through the week without embarrassing myself I could hardly imagine. I started to think of Bernard as a man who might rescue me from myself. I became more and more sure that he was everything Misty said he was. No one could describe her as a fool. Indeed she seemed more 'switched on' than I had ever seen her – almost born anew and vibrant. As though that sweet and gentle exterior we all knew and loved had been a heavy disguise now cast aside in this adventurous moment. At twenty-two, and later than most people, she seemed to become infectiously adolescent, and I more troubled than I can remember. How the hell had I got myself in this fix?

My would-be rescuer and hero was having some trouble recovering from a hangover brought on by one too many 'soothers' as he battled with his nerves the previous evening. The idea was that he would collect us at the airport and then drive us to our hotel where we could chat for a bit and then set some kind of agenda. Nothing had really been stated about what I should be doing or how I should act. Was I meant to hang around as they folded themselves into each other's arms, coughing in subtle disapproval? I really had no idea.

The idea of me being there at all now seemed sillier and sillier and ill-thought out. When Margaret and David had suggested it, especially when Katie was going as well, everything seemed to make perfect and mature sense. Now I was miles away from their influence and having to make decisions on the spur of the moment in a situation without precedent. I was not a free spirited man, although I might be a slightly grubby opportunist and this 'thinking on the hoof' business was well outside my area of comfort.

As the plane taxied along the runway, Misty suddenly turned to me, and placing her soft hand on my cheek said, "You are going to look after me aren't you, Bill?"

It was as if I had been sucked into a whirlpool, and I could only stammer, "Of course."

I felt unmasked. I probably was unmasked, and she had read my thoughts and desires with an ease which left me transfixed and uncertain on how to act. As always, silence is the last weapon of the socially desperate and I clung to it as I put my stuff away. I turned my thoughts back towards Katie and David and Margaret Potts and everything I loved back home. I suspected that I had landed myself out of my depth and was now horribly outnumbered by my 'charges.' If anything, Misty seemed to be finding my position amusing and was toying with me for reasons of her own.

I don't know if you've ever been with anyone and they have suddenly started acting in ways beyond anything you suspected in their character. That's where I was, desperately trying to make sense of a situation where the person in my charge, as it were, seemed a lot more aware and wilful than anyone would have expected. Any sense of being in control of the situation had left me as her hand touched my cheek. That steady boring man whom David trusted to protect his daughter from herself and any strange men she might meet seemed a distant illusion now. It took all my power to seem disinterested, and even then, I was pretty sure she knew how I felt. People use the word 'nightmare' loosely, but I really did feel I was in one. As we shuffled down the plane and then waited for our bags, the conversation thankfully returned to normal, led by her.

"What was the weather like outside? Will he be on time? How far is it to the hotel?" and other neutral questions two secure acquaintances might ask each other. I babbled my answers and tried to concentrate on looking for the bags. Having something mundane and responsible to do was like a rest from examination by emotional torture, and I wanted it to last as long as possible.

I texted David as I had promised to do. "Arrived Safely. Misty happy, and all is well."

Don't you love the way you can tell the truth and give entirely the wrong impression. If I could just get to my room and spend some time alone I might recover, but I had promised David that I would not leave Misty and Bernard alone until I was quite sure he was a decent man. This was not going to be easy.

Outside the airport, Bernard was parking his car and, in a mood which mirrored my own, felt almost sick with the combination of hangover and nerves. He looked at himself in the mirror and adjusted his wig to make sure it was perfectly straight. Without the perspective of a photograph it looked more stupid than ever, but what was he to do? He could not look at himself for long without a feeling of nausea sweeping through him, and horrifically, the desire to throw up pulsed through his gut. Finally, he could not help himself and leaned out of the car spattering his vomit on the concrete by the driver door.

A voice spoke out of nowhere and said, "You can't leave that mess here, mate," and he raised his eyes to see some security guy looking at him from a few yards away. This was the last thing he needed, but he just nodded his assent. He found some old newspaper in the trunk of his car and proceeded to wipe the mess up under the watchful eye of security. Fragments of his intelligence were aware of the need to stay calm, but mostly, waves of panic and emotion swept over him. He still felt clammy and generally unwell. That sweet and blessed girl with whom he'd been so free and confident online, in person now seemed to be nothing less than some avenging angel who could see inside him to his soiled and unventilated core. He cringed physically at the prospect of the meeting but somehow found the will to put one foot in front of the other.

Despite all that had happened, he just could not fail to meet her at the airport. She had come so far to see him. He still hoped against hope that when he looked into her eyes he would see that sweet being so captivated by his music as he hoped she, in looking at him, might see the man whose sensibilities had taken her beyond the normal. As he left the shelter of the car park and allowed the sun to pour down on his unsheltered head, he felt the clamminess renew around his neck and forehead and without thinking moved his hand across his brow.

As arranged, we waited for him at the arrivals point in the airport. He was not there when we got there, but patience was not a problem. I, myself, was not feeling in control of things, but Misty seemed to be brimming with excitement and no doubt saw herself as being at the gates of some great adventure. I am, I like to think, a caring man when it comes to viewing others, but even I had some trouble making sense of the figure walking towards us who was undoubtedly Bernard. The gait was far from confident, but, more striking, he seemed to have on some kind of wig which he wore crookedly across his brow. The parting, which I presume was meant to go down the left centre of his head in the normal manner, started on the left but ended up on the right side of the right eyebrow. It is hard to express in words, but I'm sure you get the general idea. Poor old Bernard was now so full of panic and unease that he had failed to check his appearance after wiping his brow. It was not a good start.

I looked at Misty to see how she was taking this, and she seemed to be smiling, but in a slightly crazy way, as though she was watching a film and some oddball character had staggered out of the crowd.

"Hello," he said nervously, as he arrived beside us.

There was an unmistakable stench of vomit around his person, and it was clear that things were not going as well for Bernard as he might have hoped. Everything rested on the response of Misty which was not long in coming.

"What's happened to your hair, Bernard?" she asked, prompting him to raise his hand to his wig and discover its new position on his head.

Without a mirror it was not easy to correct the matter, but he did as well as he could. I don't pretend to understand her workings at this time, but she seemed more amused than anything. Poor old Bernard's mouth was flapping weakly like a fish starved of water, but no words were audible.

At last he said, "We'd better go. I'll take you to your hotel."

As you'd expect, I sat in the back with Misty and Bernard, the newly joined couple sitting together in the front. I'm not sure if you know of that sub-psychic moment when someone says the worst thing they could or asks the most difficult question. I've witnessed it on occasion, and here was another instance.

Misty said, probably trying to ease the atmosphere, "And how is your grandmother keeping? I'm looking forward to seeing her."

It would be an exaggeration to say the car swerved over the road, but I saw Bernard's hands grip around the steering wheel as though he was trying to hold on against some tsunami.

"She's OK," he said, but his voice carried no conviction and a strange and awkward silence fell on the car.

I was still in the grip of the emotion started by her soft hand on my cheek, but even I could see that things had not gone as Misty must have envisaged when she started her journey. Apart from anything else, there was a gaunt and slightly leathery lined quality in his face which spoke of years somewhere older than his published age. His wig, still slightly crooked after another attempt to straighten it in the rear view mirror suggested significant baldness beneath its cover. All in all the difference between this man and the person described so gushingly to her friends was disorientating. I had no idea what to say.

Misty had now started smirking and that also made me uneasy. More and more the girl was acting in ways which had never been considered likely by her nearest and dearest. It was hard to guess, at this stage, what was going through her head.

When we got out of the car, poor old Bernard looked like a man given the simple choice between the rope and the firing squad, and his eyes were both flat and without optimism. No one looking at him could have been unsympathetic, except Misty. I don't really know what she was thinking, but I am guessing the sheer adventure of being away from home and free of normal controls was still painting the whole scene in a unique gloss. Her ability to swerve between one emotional state and another was something I was not used to at this stage. My sweet, darling, intoxicating, pliant, and gentle girl was revealed as quite another character once free of those she spent all day impressing. At least that is my theory.

As we arrived at the hotel, a pleasant modern place, I sent a quick text to David saying, "Arrived at the hotel. All good," which I hoped might reassure him.

We moved inside with our bags and registered. Myself and Misty were in adjoining rooms on the third floor and soon, as is the custom, we all proceeded to go up to them and say how nice they were. What was interesting, was there seemed to have been no move towards intimacy of expression of any kind between the couple. It might have been the smell, which was more pronounced inside the building, or embarrassment over the wig, but Bernard was getting more awkward by the minute and Misty more detached. I was, of course, uneasy, and not sure what to make of events. Back in the lobby, we ordered coffee and settled down in some chairs to drink it.

Misty, possibly now more collected after the initial shock, said, "Bernard, do you always wear that wig?"

Things were not going well for him, and his complexion could not have got any paler as he said, "No."

What was the point in denying it now?

"You might as well take it off, then," she said, and she seemed to be stifling a laugh.

I have no idea what was going through her head. Whether it was anger or amusement or disgust. Whatever it was, she was disturbingly in control of her emotions and made no move to comfort her new beau.

It is almost hard to write about it now, but the discomfort and sheer wretchedness of the man opposite me was something I had never got anywhere near witnessing before. It was a sort of slow motion horror story. Sure enough, as if he had no choice, Bernard removed his wig to reveal the bald, jug eared man of indeterminate age whom she had travelled half way across the globe to see. His destruction seemed complete.

"We'd better get to bed now," said Misty. "What time are you going to pick us up tomorrow?"

Even I was not dense enough to miss that she included me in her plans. Things were changing by the second, and it was clear, for the moment at least, that she had no intention of going anywhere without me being by her side.

Bernard rose awkwardly, clutching his now obsolete wig in his hand. He was a picture of misery, and I, for one, could not imagine him wanting to come back for another day of torture at her hands. There was a cool, knowing professionalism about her treatment of him which was both impressive and chilling. This demure acolyte had changed, in these new circumstances into an assured and practised social operative. There was nothing shy about her manner with him, and any anger she felt was implicit rather than expressed. She had become someone you would not want to get on the wrong side of, and that was a new view of her to say the least.

After he left, having agreed to come back again about midday the next day, with a friend he thought we might like to meet, Misty suggested we have a quick drink at the bar before retiring.

You remember me saying that drunks never lie, but often lose the ability to control their tongue? I was very aware of that now, but tried to act as though I hadn't a care in the world. She ordered a wine and I got myself a beer. We looked at each other, and I don't know why, just started to giggle.

"He's really very odd," I said, and remember I was stone-cold sober.

"How old do you think he is?" she replied. "He looks about the same age as my Dad."

Getting more careless now as the mood of conspirators gripped us I said, "I think he'd just been sick. Not your normal strategy with a new girl," and she smiled at me as if discovering a friend.

"You're so much fun when you're on your own. I've never seen you when Katie is not around you," and I smiled, feeling somehow liberated by her approval.

"It's almost like being out of school isn't it?" I said and we both laughed again.

"One more for the road, or the stairs at least, or do we go off sensibly to sleep?"

"I don't want to be sensible," she said, and smiled at me as though I was her new best friend and conspirator. The odd thing was Bernard hardly featured in our conversation.

We forged a quick alliance by comparing ourselves to two victims bossed around by the same head of drama. Better men than I would have felt disloyal, but I was too full of excitement to worry about niceties. To have this vision of soft, beautiful sexiness laugh at my comments and sit near me as though we were new best friends was so intoxicating that I hardly needed any drink to lose my sense of decorum or bearings. I behaved myself, in part at least, but my head was all over the place. I couldn't really work out how a girl who had been so determined to come out here and meet the man she loved could be so detached when he appeared not to be all he had suggested on his profile.

Finally I couldn't hold myself back and just said, "Misty, I can't work out why you are not more upset that Bernard is a little different to the man you thought he was."

"A little different?" she said and raised her eyebrows in a new and comic manner.

I burst out laughing and sprayed a mouthful of beer over my trousers.

"Mucky boy," she said, and I just replied that it wasn't my fault.

All the stresses in my relations with her, or lack of them, seemed to have vanished, and for the first time in as long as I could remember, I was sitting on my own with a girl I hardly knew and knew too well, chatting as though we were joint conspirators on some fantastic adventure, and of course, we were. At last, we agreed that sleep was a necessity and went up to our rooms. Her room was the one before mine so I waited while she undid her door. Without embarrassment, she turned around and threw her arms around me kissing me on the cheek.

"I'm just so pleased you are here, Bill. It's the best thing ever," and with that she turned and closed the door.

Chapter Eleven

Given my feelings about her, and the general sense of disorientation, what with jet-lag, being on a new continent, and the very strange appearance of her boyfriend, you can imagine my head was spinning at some speed as I laid it on the pillow. I should have been sleeping, and finally did, but before then, I floated off on this amazing and unknown experience of feeling free in the company of someone from the opposite sex. Someone so full of life and pretty and sexy and now mischievous. Would the real Misty please come out and say hello to the world? If this was her, I was beside myself with excitement. Furthermore, she seemed to like me, calling me her 'fellow conspirator' and us 'the naughty ones.' I can't fully define or explain either of these two expressions, but they both gave me the glow – that floating feeling when you stumble unexpectedly and find yourself in paradise. At the very least, I had a whole week with her, and all the money a man could want, thanks to my father who would be deeply disgusted by my behaviour.

With a new found freedom and recklessness, I looked up at the ceiling and said "Love you, Dad," before smiling and turning my head to rest on the pillow. Tomorrow was going to be the grandest day ever.

Over in another part of town, Bernard was feeling quite differently about events. There is a theory – it may be mine, I'm not sure – that some lives seem constructed for the amusement of others. At this moment it looked as if Bernard fit this description beautifully, and like all such people, promptly rung the worst person he could chose to tell them about the airport meeting.

"Brilliant!" said Derek. "I'm coming right over."

Sure enough, within twenty minutes he was at Bernard's door with a bottle of Jack Daniels.

When Bernard opened the door he felt empty inside and without initiative.

"Hi, mate," he said with a stab at normalcy, but otherwise hardly seemed present in the room.

"So tell me all about it," said Derek, growing brighter by the minute.

This story was getting better and better, and when Bernard told him about being sick and the wig being crooked, life could hardly get richer for Bernard's closest friend.

"Have you told her about the grandmother or your kids yet, mate?" and Bernard just nodded 'no' and took another sip of Jack Daniels.

In the circumstances, gliding outside a few glasses of JD was not the wisest thing to do at this hour, but Bernard and Wisdom now seemed distant relatives.

At last Derek 'stepped up to the plate' for one motive or another, and said. "Look here, I'm coming to the hotel with you tomorrow. It's best you don't face her on your own, and I may be able to help you."

Bernard, so drunk on liquor and disaster that his judgement had collapsed, just nodded. Within a few short hours his dream that this sweet girl who 'got' his soul so well and made him feel whole when the world beyond ignored him, had morphed into some direct and judging being who made him wriggle on her gaze. That he was the author of his own misfortune, he understood, but he also longed for a little understanding. Perhaps, he thought, with his friend to steady him, and after a good night's sleep, he might be able to face the situation more squarely and rescue his romance. His thought was more of style than conviction, but by now, he had lost all direction and his pride. Derek, replete with a tale which was better than any he could have expected, arranged to meet him at eleven the next morning and took his leave. A little drunk driving seemed a small matter in the circumstances.

The truth about Bernard, when I thought about him after the event, is that he was far from being a bad man. He could be described as a good man by those not seeking a romantic connection with him. He was loyal, faithful, and honest in his work, which offered some scope for corrupt practices he never considered, and he was gentle and observant of those around him who were more frail than himself. He never proactively set out to harm anyone, and on many measurements stood out as a better man than many: gentler, more understanding, and forgiving, honest about himself, and reliable as an employee. It was only this lack of tender recognition, or whatever you seek to call it, which proved his undoing. Anyone he met, from his wife through to his boss was more interested in him as a utility than as a being with feelings and value. It left him with a need he could only articulate through deceit, but it was never his intention to harm.

His ex-wife, whom he had betrayed so scandalously some might say, was herself a hard, self-centred women whose sense of intimacy was best expressed by sharing a biscuit, and for whom 'doing your duty' was the highest compliment you could pay a person. Especially, it must be said, if 'doing your duty' happened to coincide with being useful to her. None of this seemed to help Bernard now. No sudden wind of change or miracle phone call sounded to save his fate. Misty did not lie in her hotel bed and reflect on the sweet desperation in his eyes as he removed the wig before her. In fact, with a disturbingly easy change of emotional direction, she was now seeing the adventure in quite another light and relished the chance to spread her wings and enjoy herself in the company of a man she both trusted to look after her and not get between her and new experiences, namely me. Derek was far too amused by the story to waste any time on sympathy. It is possible he felt a level of venom that Bernard had found this girl without consulting him, and then partly upstaged him with Samantha. He never voiced any such thoughts, but he was a man used to orchestrating events rather than observing them.

~2~

In the morning, I felt surprisingly refreshed, and as I was walking out of the shower, there was a sudden and loud banging on the door. Puzzled and slightly unnerved I went to open it, and there was Misty, already dressed and beaming saying, "Hurry up, lazy bones. Let's go and have a look see before Bernard gets here. I wonder what the breakfasts are like."

"Alright, bossy," I replied, and she laughed and then bowed slightly as if introducing her new personality. She seemed alight with good humour and cheer and like a girl on her first holiday away from her parents.

"Do you want coffee or tea?" she said. "I'll go down and order breakfast while you try and get dressed."

She started to giggle. Almost anything seemed to amuse her and her sense of celebration was infectious. Poor old Bernard seemed not to be on her mind, and was far from mine as I revelled in her intoxicating attentions. I texted David to tell him that Misty was in good form and had slept well and that we were meeting for breakfast. Bernard was due at 12 am our time.

Soon, I got the familiar ping noise and saw his reply, "Thanks for looking after her. Try not to let her out of your sight. Katie sends her love."

I looked at the message for a second, almost disorientated as if it had come from another life before this new existence. These nervous concerns about Misty from her small community in England seemed exaggerated and of little consequence when you saw how happy she was. The main purpose of our trip seemed to be changing. Still, ever dutiful as I sat down to eat opposite her, she looked quietly stunning in some floaty, pink blouse and jeans. I asked her if she had any thought about Bernard.

"Well, he's not who I thought he was," she said, "but I'm not going to allow it to spoil my holiday."

Behind the smile there was a hint of flintiness which was disconcerting, but as her new confidant and best friend, I paid it little attention. On reflection, I think she was more angry than anything, but she was hard to read. Maybe she felt she might have made a fool of herself, and been too trusting and feared the teasing and the telling off she would get when she returned home. She was more than glad that I was there without Katie and her passing judgements. She could see how much it meant for me to spend time with her, and she felt safe. She would see Bernard because she said she would, but really she had already turned her back on him.

How the great love story had crumbled so easily at the first hurdle, to mix a couple of metaphors, I've no idea, but it had. Possibly, the worship of a young lady for her first beau is a brittle thing and fractures easily under pressure. I think, sad as it is to say it, that, in this case, appearances really did matter, and the new bald Bernard with the lined and pale face framed by those unfortunate jug ears was just a step too far for a girl who had fallen in love with a sweet and gifted musical spirit whose face was framed in beautiful, soft, brown hair. She remembered saying to him, after he'd sent her a batch of new photographs, that she could not wait to run her fingers through it, and he had seemed a bit awkward about the idea. At the time, she took it for a pleasing shyness, but now she had a clearer understanding of the situation. She wondered what else he had to tell her.

When Bernard and Derek turned up in the hotel lobby, Bernard seemed edgy and uneasy, as you might imagine, and slightly surprising with his honest baldness, but Derek had that chirpy uninhibited manner adopted by a successful insurance salesman and introduced himself before anyone could speak. It is a fact of life that a certain kind of man – smooth, practised, and over debonair who has an acknowledged record 'with the ladies' – can be an object of some revulsion to those women not swept away by a 'charm' they see as creepy. One thing was quite clear,

Misty was at this meeting more as a result of momentum and good manners than because she thought the romance was going anywhere, and for Derek to introduce himself as Bernard's closest friend before rewarding Misty and myself with a wink, was the approach least likely to win her over. For Bernard, I still felt real compassion, and I could sense a decent man lived within the profile now so disastrously illuminated. The worst thing he could have done, if he sought to redeem himself, was bring Derek with him, but poor Bernard was beyond all sense by this time and was moved blindly by some instinct unexplained.

I almost tried to help him. When I caught his eye I smiled at him and even got a brief recognition a drowning man might give you before vanishing beneath the waves: a look of common humanity, but one marked by the knowledge that he was beyond your help. Derek was quite another matter and was just out to impress.

Trying to clear up exactly who Bernard was, Misty suddenly asked Bernard, "How far away is your grandmother?"

Before he could say anything, Derek stuck his reply in saying starkly, "There is no grandmother. It was just a marketing ploy, but he's a good bloke. You can be sure about that." He spoke as if the whole thing was amusing and we were all 'people of the world.'

It might be that the remark was intended to be helpful, and I don't think it was technically possible for Bernard to look any paler than he did. I just sat there stunned, puzzled, embarrassed, and slightly elated. Why I should be elated, I had no idea, but the emotion did me little credit.

Misty suddenly stood up and said to Bernard, "Can you come outside with me alone for a second?"

This made me uneasy because it left me on my own with Derek, whose company was some distance from enjoyable. Fortunately, he seemed quite unaware of that and asked me what I intended to do with myself while the love birds were out on the town 'or elsewhere.' His inference was obvious, and I determined to ignore it.

"I've got books to read," I said, and then looked at the door hoping that Bernard and Misty would return immediately from their first face-to-face conversation.

Instead, I saw Misty come back alone, and without preamble she said, "Bernard's waiting for you outside." To me she said, "Shall we be off?" Without further ceremony she walked off towards the lift.

I followed her, of course, and with the new freedom her warmth had granted to me said, "Spill the beans."

"Look," she replied, "we can have loads of fun here on our own away from the parents and Katie, and I don't want those saddos ruining it."

This sounded a bit harsh to me, but I've often witnessed people denying a decision they've made, which later turns out to have been unwise or show them in poor light.

She slipped her hand through my arm and said, "Where shall we go?"

Remember that my bank account was recently swelled by the ambivalent generosity of my deceased father, and I spoke with abandon and confidence.

"There is a Michelin-starred restaurant here, and I suggest we go there straight away and start this adventure in style."

"Oh, Bill, you're brilliant. Let's get ready and go."

It was one of those days when the sun shone with perfect light, where birds sang with just the right resonance, and even the mundane seemed to glow with a beauty unimaginable in any other circumstances. She smiled at me and laughed at my asides and sometimes even squeezed my arm and pressed herself against me as we walked. We rediscovered the child within each other and in our circumstances. Here, almost by fate and various accidents, two people who would never have been alone were just that, and far away from those who presumed the right to tell us how to live our lives. We had time, money, and each other, and nothing could prevent us enjoying ourselves and celebrating the moment.

I kept some small reserve and even though I was boiling with the desire to kiss her, I clung to my controlled exterior. I say

I did, but if you heard me whinnying at her jokes or observations you would have wondered 'Who is this man?' We felt the couple of the day. So charmed by life that I saw people turn to look at us as we walked, and smile at what they saw. The fates would brook no barrier to our joy and, astonishing as it was, a late cancellation at the restaurant saw us sitting at a beautiful table by the window. The waiter seemed intent on sharing our happiness and doing all he could to make it richer. We sat there sipping pina coladas, because they seemed so much fun and studying the menu.

"We can eat anything we want. We can do anything we want," I said to her and the world, though no one else was listening. She gave me a smile which took me towards paradise.

She, herself, seemed so happy and so full of joy that I was drunk on her gaze. Somewhere at the back of my intellect a voice asked how she could have turned her back on Bernard so easily and switched her attention to me in this way, but I was too in love to care. I can say that now. She had finally liberated me to tell the truth, and hopefully, she had found hers, that here was a man who would protect and celebrate her all her life. Our smiles were without embarrassment and, unconsciously, our hands met in the middle of the table.

When you pay a great deal of money for a meal, you can spend a long time eating it and no one seems to mind. We drank champagne, although neither of us especially liked it, because it seemed to be the drink of the day. We ordered a very expensive bottle because that made us laugh, and even the waiter shared our joke. We ate truffles because they were impossibly expensive and that seemed to have amused us as well. We both said how bossy and controlling Katie was and how her parents wouldn't let her have any fun. She said she was bored with being a 'goody two-shoes,' and now she just wanted to experience life.

"We can do anything you want, darling," I said.

The word just slipped out, but she just said, "Am I your darling, Bill? Is that who I am?"

And I, lost and drunk in love, just said, "You're everything."

Those minor details which breathed of a life back home – my wife and her cousin, plus her mum and dad, and anyone else you can think of – no longer had a voice or we a conscience on that level. We felt like prisoners just released, and we would not be limited by formalities. For now, we held each other's gaze and the opportunity. We required nothing else.

Slightly drunk, but not too much, we spent the afternoon walking round the zoo. We had no such things in our small community, and just to see the lions and the elephants filled us with amazement. Her hand always on my arm, we shared our observations with each other and discovered a deep and passionate shared interest in wildlife. We were discovering a deep and shared interest in almost everything till we were mildly spooked. The chances that we, two people from the same community but separated by conventions and family ties should find themselves out here, and discovering so many shared interests and attitudes seemed like some divine orchestration, the chances of it happening so slim that only some deliberation of the fates would have made it possible and we were determined not to let them down.

After a while, she said she was a bit tired and would like to go back for a nap before the evening. I felt the same way, jet lag perhaps, and I acknowledged that to her. On the road outside we hailed a taxi and went off to the hotel. There was a sort of atmosphere in the lift, not easy to describe. I felt everything for her, but good manners – or was it self-preservation – restrained me. Is that the right description? Or was I awkward, shy, or principled? Or is that unlikely?

Reaching her door, she opened it and turned to me, saying in a softer, shyer, sweeter voice than normal, "I don't want to say goodbye," and I found myself inside her room and kissing her.

Melting is a word some people use, and now I know why. Our clothes fell off, or so it seemed, between the kissing and soon we were naked and on the bed. I treasured her so much that, even though I was hungry, I was gentleness itself with this sweet girl who gave herself to me.

Afterwards, as we lay in each other's arms and her soft blue eyes shined into mine I said, "We've got a bit of explaining to do."

Her look clouded for a second, and she said, "How?"

I raised the duvet, and sure enough, among the normal mess was a patch of blood which marked the passing of her virginity. Looking at it she smiled again, and seemed to find it funny.

"Oops," she said and we both laughed again, and held each other before the kisses performed their natural magic. Finally, we drifted off to sleep, two innocents careless of their crimes and discarded responsibilities.

~3~

In another part of town Bernard was in quite another light, untouched by magic and sat alone in his room wondering how it was that his sweet girl, who made his world complete, had changed into this brittle and judging thing.

As they walked out of the hotel and stood outside, she had not asked for an explanation, or put her hand upon his arm and said "I understand," raised herself on tiptoe and kissed his cheek.

She had just looked at him, as though he was something infinitely discardable, and said, "Fuck off," and that was all she said.

Before he'd opened his mouth, her back was receding through the door and he was not to see her again, or so he thought.

Derek drove him home and hardly noticed his silence, "Win some, lose some," was the nearest to comforting he went.

He had some sense that this was an event beyond the ordinary for Bernard, but he just couldn't be doing with people going soggy over girls. The only one he treasured was his sister, and he never thought of her at times like this.

As they reached the lodgings, Bernard said he wanted to be alone and fair enough.

Derek drove off saying, "See you soon, mate," but there was something in Bernard's movement which suggested his company would not be sought in the near future. Derek shook his head. He'd never made a mistake as far as he knew, but there was no allowing for the way some people behaved.

Sitting on his bed, Bernard sought for some understanding but found none. The afternoon stretched into the early evening, and he realised no one would call. He checked his emails to see if she had thought again, and written to him once more; those sweet sentences which gave him dignity.

As he was checking his emails, she was lying in my arms, drunk on love and new discoveries. We slept like tender lambs. A cliché never seemed to hold such truth as at this time when my whole being sang. There I go again, but who can blame me. Life had granted me my deepest wish.

Bernard moved to the piano for no reason and began to express his lament musically as his hands drifted up and down the keyboard. He was at that place called despair, where nothing positive remains, and the future is shaped by instinct without apparent direction. The mood rose up within him, filling his eyes with water until at last he opened his mouth and began to sing:

"I moved to kiss her, but she turned away.

The sun, it would not shine that day.

The birds were silent in the trees;

I begged for love upon my knees."

He paused to write the passage down and then continued until a new song sat on the paper beside him. Something in his creation gave him purpose, and he moved uncertainly out of desolation to a place where he might express himself. With no one else to talk to, the piano became his only outlet, and he spoke to it shamelessly, more nakedly than he had ever done before.

Back at the hotel, we were now waking from our slumber, unaware of the sense of tragedy her discarded lover was experiencing elsewhere in the city, or the thoughts of our relatives back home.

Reaching for my phone, I checked my messages and saw that David had already sent four of them, starting with, "How's it going?" Through to, "Is everything OK?" and finally "I'm getting worried."

I'm not proud of myself, but what I did was turn my phone off and shelve that problem for a later time.

Holding Misty to myself, and wondering at her open nakedness I said. "No point in huddling in these little rooms. Why don't we get a suite?"

"Oh, Bill," she said, "can we really?" and you can guess at my reply. Her father must be dealt with, but for now, I would not let his shadow mark the day.

The suite, when we took it – and on magic days like this, all things seemed possible – was beyond anything our ordered imaginations could conceive. It had its own sitting room and a bathroom with two baths.

"We won't need two of those," she said naughtily when she saw them, and I was beside myself with joy.

I cannot speak for her, but she seemed as transported as I, and I suppose I must admit, she was getting everything she wanted from a man who loved her more than life or his reputation.

Thoughts of her Dad kept filtering into my head, and finally I said, "Do you think we should tell your Dad?"

"Not today, Bill. Just say we are Ok, because we are, aren't we, Bill?" and I moved to kiss her once again.

Her sweet, soft lips opened up to mine, and then I spoke.

"We'll always be OK, Misty. I'll love you all my life."

And she just said, "And I you."

Without compunction I typed in the words, "Sorry, David. Been pretty hectic here, and my phone was dead, but all OK. Misty is happy and safe, and I'm keeping her in my sight."

I don't know what time it was back home but straight away came the reply, "Keep your phone charged, you silly bugger. Glad everything OK."

So it was on this day and the next. We drowned ourselves in treats and intimacy. For someone inexperienced, she had the touch of a magician, and I experienced pleasures and release beyond that I thought possible. We made each other laugh and shared discoveries as freely as the wind. No secrets now. We talked a lot of Katie and Misty's dad, and how they both controlled us in their way. Whatever my new relationship with his daughter, he remained the man I respected above all others, and whose good wishes I valued above all else. About Katie I had no clear idea, but I was dimly aware that I must face her somehow, some way, but not now.

Both Misty and I were growing more and more certain of each other. I always was, of course, but for Misty, this was a new experience. You know the way new lovers and old acquaintances share their preconceptions of each other? We did that at length, although I was more discrete about the longevity of my lust. Somehow, that might not have moved her as I wished, but she talked freely of myself. Of how I seemed so henpecked and care-worn but loved by her mum and dad. How I made people laugh and looked out for them, but never made any demands for myself.

She said to me, staring at me with those young eyes, which hardly knew what pain was and said, "I'm with you now, Bill. You'll never be alone," and I'm embarrassed to say I felt my eyes water, and she called me a fool and brushed the tears away with such gentleness. What would Derek have made of such a simple scene? I dare not think. Two people drunk on love who promise each other more than they can give.

As part of our growing commitment, we agreed we must sit down that day and Skype with her mum and dad. They needed to know the situation and for us to declare our love for each other before the world and them. Difficulties could be ironed out later, I thought, referring to my wife and their niece. My sincerity would win then over I was sure.

Chapter Twelve

I messaged David to say we would Skype him at 11am his time which was 7pm our time. We were off to some art gallery in the afternoon, and we should be well-rested before we made the call. In truth, although we had been to the zoo, theatre, and other locations, we were more interested, at that time, in revelling in the luxury of our hotel and exploring each other to worry about much else. We felt the need to do something normal with our days, so we would have something to tell the folks, but what we truly wanted was each other, and the secret world we were creating.

I had texted David regularly but, lacking concrete information, his texts had taken on a slightly urgent edge and both Misty and I agreed that now was the time to have the talk.

I was nervous. I was very nervous, but I knew my love for Misty was real and that together we could surmount any difficulty.

The call, when it began was not easy. We were sitting in the living room area of our suite and Misty's hand was in mine as she squeezed up beside me. I'm not sure if she had fully thought through the subtleties of our situation, but she was not acting as though she had. There, in front of us, sat David and Margaret Potts, her mum and dad, and in some way my mentors, in surroundings very familiar to us. It made the situation more real and finite, but I steeled myself to control my emotions. Misty spoke first because, frankly, I had failed.

"We're a couple, Dad. We're in love, and I want you to be happy for us."

Margaret, who always got to the heart of the matter without any difficulty said, "Does Katie know?" and Misty sort of giggled. I'm not sure if it was genuine amusement or if she, herself, was becoming nervous.

Whatever the situation, I knew I had to speak or I would lose standing in her eyes. I managed to control my voice and speaking as steadily as I could said, "I know it's a surprise, but I truly love her, and I will look after her."

Misty leaned over and gave me a kiss when I said that, but Margaret, in an uncharacteristically sour comment said, "Is that what you told Katie's mum when you seduced her daughter?" and then David started.

He still had the Lennon glasses and the multi-coloured jacket, but somehow, he seemed a different man. I could see the anger building in him, and that was something I'd never witnessed before. Now they were both looking at me, or that is how it seemed.

"I trusted you, Bill. I trusted you with my daughter, and look where we are now. You've betrayed myself and Margaret, and Katie and her mum and dad without a backward glance."

I kept my poise somehow or other and replied, "You trusted me, David, and you were right to do so. I know it's a shock but we truly love each other, and all other matters will be dealt with in due course."

"Have you told Katie?" injected Margaret. I had never seen her so disturbed and her anger, again, was unprecedented.

David continued, "You're living life backwards, mate."

"What do you mean?" I asked. I had not come across the description.

"I mean you left here behaving like an adult, and now you're acting like a spoiled kid, and smashing everything you can get your hands on."

"It's not like that at all," I said, but found I was talking to a blank screen.

It was hard to know what to say or think. I had never seen either of them so angry, and it was hard to ignore the fact that all their anger was directed at me, or that they felt I had betrayed them. I have noticed in the past that, sometimes, in order to preserve your love for someone, you direct all feelings of anger onto another person involved in the story. That was clearly my situation, and I would have to bare it.

Misty and I looked at each other, and then something remarkable happened. She leaned forward, pressed herself into me and kissed me slow and hard.

When we separated she said, "You're the man I love, and they will see that in the end. Even Katie will get used to the new arrangement. I'm proud of you, what you've just done and who you are."

I was so stunned at her reply. Her style was so considered and mature I had trouble associating it with my naughty friend and darling, but we seldom examine the source of praise and I was in no mood to so now.

To have her response be the best that any man could imagine in my circumstances sent me over the edge and I heard myself saying, "Let's go and buy a ring. I know we can't get married yet, but we will."

Her eyes told me all I needed to know, and then her voice said yes. It is a moment I will treasure all my life. I don't mean treasure, although I'd like to, but it's certainly a moment I will remember all my life.

What it was or how it was I didn't know, but I was, or seemed to be, her new statement of independence from her mum and dad, from Katie, and from others who had treated her as a pet. She had found a man of means, who would stand by her and love her come what may. She no longer had to play the demure virgin. She was becoming a fully-fledged adult in front of my eyes, late in the day by most standards, but at a speed which would have surprised anybody. I over analyse things and, at this stage, my darling remained delightfully enigmatic to me on some levels. I suspect we both may have been passengers of her emotions. I did not care. I was too busy enjoying them to worry over-much about their origins.

Easy plans and easy money are a flammable mix, and soon, we were making arrangements faster than you can blink an eyelid. Returning back to her, or our, home was clearly out of the question, so with the studied abandon of one for whom money is little more than a vulgar utility, I booked two flights, first class of course, to Birmingham. Possibly, my aunt would put us up, but there were a wealth of good hotels where we might rest until we got our bearings. So as a precaution, I booked a suite at one of the city's best. That dull job done, we put all concerns aside and continued to enjoy our break, as it had become.

As long as Misty was not concerned by events, I was not either. I had everything I wanted in my arms, and other matters could wait. Katie, languishing in bed with her broken leg and with knowledge that her husband had seduced her best friend and cousin was not a concern at this stage. We became figures fuelled by whims and sampling what the city had to offer. Nothing was too expensive or unusual for us. Anything was available as long as it made my darling happy.

I suggested, in a moment of empathy, that it might be a kindness to see Bernard once more before we left, and to my surprise, she agreed. More than that, her eyes shone and she smiled at me.

"That's what I love about you, Bill. You have the generous thoughts other people don't have. I wish my mum and dad could hear you now."

I smiled and banked the praise. In fact, I'd had so much admiration, I hardly knew where to put the stuff but it made me feel like a lord. As long as I had Misty, I was sure I could conquer any difficulty and show compassion and understanding to those who stood in my way. I was discovering a new higher being within myself, but less monk-like than the old model. This new man had beauty on his arm and in his bed, and the money to guild her life with luxury and yet the humanity to spare time for those less fortunate than himself. I started to love this new man and revelled in my new persona.

Bernard, when Misty spoke to him, was more sanguine than I would have expected and suggested we come over to his place. He gave us the address. I am guessing he was beyond pretence now and just wanted to be himself. He had nothing else left. We arrived at his lodgings which were not derelict, but otherwise seemed undistinguished. He greeted us at the door, bald, jug-eared but somehow more composed. Actually, a much better meeting than any he had got near achieving at the airport or hotel. Perhaps he had underestimated himself, aided by his loyal friend. I don't think it took him very long to see that Misty had transferred her adoration to another man, and that that man was full of the joy being admired by a beauty who was so recently his. He nodded but made no sour comment or other acknowledgment of the fact.

"I suppose you want to know what I was playing at," he said to Misty. He was not hostile to me, but his gaze was firmly directed at her.

Regardless, I spoke first, "It's OK, mate, we all go off track on occasion. We just wanted to make sure you were alright."

"Very kind of you," he said, looking at me, and I caught in his voice that comments from anyone but Misty were not sought for, or appreciated.

Turning to her again, he said, "I've written a song about it. Would you like to hear it?"

She said, "Yes," and I was now wise enough to remain silent.

I suppose playing the gloating winner of the man who stole his love's heart is not an appreciated role, but I had not thought of that aspect when I suggested the visit. Little did he care.

And so he began. At the piano, he seemed quite a different man. Articulating misery and loss was his speciality, and it was clear he could do it much better than most, or anyone else I have met.

"I moved to kiss her, but she turned away," he sang, and his voice, made stronger by sincerity, stroked our emotions with each succeeding verse.

I turned to look at Misty and saw something both disturbing and moving. Tears were pouring down her cheeks in silent applause for this man who had so little and understood so much. Now it became clear why she had travelled such distances to see him. Away from everyday assessments, he clearly was extraordinary, and it showed in every note.

When he was finished, he turned from the piano, his voice calm and controlled, and said to her, "I allowed myself to play the fool, but I loved you and I always will. That is my present to you."

I had entered his rooms like an impresario, orchestrating some grand debriefing of a comic episode, but I could feel my presence vanishing into the shadows, a forgotten figure as these two souls remembered their connection.

He was right. The man he looked like would never have attracted a glance from her, but the man he was would have attracted admiration from anybody. His tragedy was that, only with her had he dared to be that man. Nothing is more powerful than sincerity, and I was silent and helpless in its company. I did not move to kiss her, as the song says, because even I realised it might not be the time.

I am just an ordinary man without a special talent or influence, and benefiting from a small inheritance that I was seeking to squander as fast as possible.

Watching these two people I could think of little to say, so I said the lamest thing I could. "What time does the art gallery close?"

They both looked at me with bewilderment. I understood. Who cared, at this moment, if there was an art gallery or what hours it opened? I sank into a silence then and awaited the outcome of the meeting.

At last, we rose to leave, and I could see that his cheeks were also damp with tears. How could I have suggested such a meeting? I realised I had been duped by his bizarre greeting at the airport into thinking there was nothing about the man, and thus suggesting the meeting on his home turf. Freed from the need to lie, his performance had been powerful and assured, and I was sensible enough just to get her out of there, and repair any damage later.

When gods become mortal, they search around for some protection, and that is how I felt now. I was cautious in my approach, but I think I struck the right note.

"You were right to love him. Despite his age and other handicaps he is an extraordinary man, and only a woman like you would notice that."

Thank goodness she turned to me and smiled, "You always see the small details which change everything."

I smiled in return but made a note to myself. I had chosen the word 'woman' over 'girl' because it showed her more respect. I was no longer floating in euphoria, but marketing myself out of some waters where rocks might break the hull of that small craft in which my future sailed.

We had left Bernard because we had to. It seemed a pre-ordained decision but it was not a clean departure. She was clearly disturbed by the meeting and in some special place to which I had no access. For the first time since our glorious union, only four days before, I felt like an outsider in the thought processes of my special darling. It was an uncomfortable awakening, and I decided that the least said about the visit, the better it would be. The hard facts are that a man who was twenty-two years older than her, with two children of his own, was unlikely to be a welcome match with her parents. The children had come to light when Misty spotted a photo of them on the shelf and asked who they were. When he told her, there was no awkwardness or embarrassment about it. He had gone too far for that now, and I realised she could not say or do nothing which might hurt him more than he had hurt himself. What was also apparent, inside the wreckage of his life, lay a talent and sensibility far from the ordinary. Free from the everyday he had been able to express it to her, and rebirth it in himself. It had been a meeting full of unexpected colours and revelations, and I would have to wait till

Misty gained some distance from its influence before I gave further attention to my intimate thoughts.

The taxi ride back to the hotel was unusually quiet, and I could see Misty pouring over the whole event in her mind. I think it possible that, for such a girl as her, the impact was too large and significant to be digested. To have the love of someone so talented, even if it was unrecognised was a tribute she had never sought, but she was powerfully moved all the same. I would have to bide my time, but I knew, for now, silence was the best strategy.

Out of her reverie, she turned to me and said, "Are you an honest man?"

It was not a settling question to someone on the back foot but I said, "Yes, I am, in important matters, and certainly when I speak about you."

I managed to look her squarely in the eye when I said it, but she received the reply, more as one taking evidence than as a besotted fiancé. The hard thing was that, unwittingly, I had placed myself and her in the company of a man who had nothing to hide, and how many of us could survive such a meeting if our own consciences are troubled.

Silence seemed called for once again.

~2~

It was one of those critical moments in a life or a relationship, and, as always seemed to be the case with me, I would have to wait on events. I was, I sadly acknowledged, one of those men who normally wait upon events rather than shape them, and here was another case in point. Perhaps sensing my disquiet, she moved her hand over mine. Relief poured through me, though I tried to remain unconcerned. Perhaps I had not lost her after all. We walked around the art gallery in near silence, but gradually the quality of the art around us took us away from self-examination to an appreciation of other things.

Here, I was on stronger and stronger ground and gradually found my voice. The Art Gallery of Western Australia, as it is known, is not generally talked of in European circles, but inside it is a treasure trove of contemporary art which can stimulate the most apathetic. Before my eyes, Misty became more animated by what she saw, and I was reborn somehow, in her eyes, as the man who made this whole adventure and her education possible. I realised my importance to her. With regard to her life, I would lay down my own, and all I had was hers. It was not a noble present perhaps, but in giving it, I was being honest about my feelings. In some disconcerting way, Misty seemed to have a nose for sincerity. She picked it up in Bernard, when unaware of his strange creations and she picked it up from me. Perhaps it was a gift inherited from her mother, but whatever it was, I felt her frame relax and her hand was once again in mine as we, explored what the gallery could offer us.

Back in the hotel, and slightly tired after our adventures and a meal we sat in our rooms and watched a film. Although still slightly pensive, she seemed to have recovered somewhat from her meeting with Bernard. I opened my laptop carelessly and had a quick look at my emails. I saw immediately that there was one from David:

Dear Bill,

I trusted you to protect my daughter, but all you have done is soil her life with your sick desires and left your wife, my niece, in tears at your betrayal and the loss of her best friend. How you have not had the courtesy to ring or write to her in any way is beyond my understanding. I pray that Misty comes back to us soon, and that you enjoy the pain and distress you so richly deserve and have given us so much of. I do not regard Misty as being at fault in this matter. As the older man, you should have had enough self-awareness and honour in you to restrain your depravity. I have shown Margaret this email and she agrees with every word. You make me ill.

David

P.S. I have sent a copy of this to Misty for her information.

I thought it better to show Misty the email straight away

rather than let her discover it. I was becoming increasingly aware of the mood back home as our return flight loomed. Misty read it quickly, and shot me a glance of some compassion.

"Poor Bill," she said. "You're certainly catching all the flack," and I smiled ruefully.

That night was the first night since we had 'discovered each other' when we were not intimate. We lay touching, but not embracing as I tried to make sense of an emotional landscape which was changing swiftly before us. That secret garden we had mutually discovered just four days before, now seemed blighted by some strange fungus, and new blooms were hard to find. More than at any time in my past, I realised that my happiness was bound up in the attitude of another whose sweet face now lay sleeping on the pillow beside me. I had been enjoying my newfound wealth, and there was no doubt it had made a difference with Misty. Now, more than ever, I was aware that money may not buy you happiness, but misery comes free of charge.

In the morning, we began to pack, and we would have time for a gentle lunch and goodbyes at the hotel before an arranged taxi took us to the airport. The duties and the packing proved to be of some relief. We were no longer in that place where you can look at each other without caution and know your standing is untarnished. Through my own stupidity in contacting Bernard and the wrath of the people back home, I had exposed myself to corrosive levels of wrath, which I could see clearly had eaten into Misty's innocent appreciation of me.

That fact that Bernard, free of hope, had turned out to be a finer man than I had previously imagined was also troubling. Was I really the noble and slightly gauche protector of her future, or were deceitful stratagems present in my approach? I feared she was not entirely sure.

On the surface, we remained warm and affectionate, and she reached up to kiss me as I moved to drag the cases out of our suite and towards the lift.

"We won't forget this trip," she said and I agreed.

There was an air of gentleness about her, of conclusion,

which quietly anaesthetised me against the shock I feared was coming. She said nothing, and was gently attentive to me but without that playful character which marks the unguarded relationship. Travel is always a burden, but especially when you stomach churns with tension. I wished there was something I could say to lighten the mood, but I feared to put another foot wrong.

More films were watched and slumbers taken. I talked about where we would live and suggested some locations to her. She listened attentively, as if searching for something in my words, but my nerve was gone. I had basked in the warmth of her attentions, but now they seemed more impersonal. I could not understand how a couple who shared such passion a few short hours before could now be so guarded with each other. No new facts had come to light. Nothing that David and Margaret said had altered the circumstances as we knew them to be, and I knew myself to be sincere, but I was now speaking to the wind. Other interested parties had left the courtroom and only sentencing remained.

When she said me to in the arrivals area of the airport that she thought it better if she went straight on home and talked to her parents, I agreed, of course. Good manners were all I had left, and I clung to them with pious misery. Outside the airport, I walked her to a taxi and asked the driver to take her to Birmingham International where trains for the southwest were readily available. I gave her money for the journey and saw her settle in the cab.

Grabbed by emotion, I leaned inside and said, "I love you with all my heart. You know that, darling."

And she just said, "I know." The cab drew away, and I stood staring at it as it turned the corner. She did not turn to look at me.

She had not said, "I love you, too."

I had nothing now but my bags and the address of some hotel. I had booked a suite, of course, because that was what besotted couples do, but was I now in a couple? I would change it for a room if I could.

Chapter Thirteen

The suite, when I looked around it, was large and built to impress the impressionable. For me, it was a vast impersonal expanse, but I could imagine looking round it with Misty. Peering into cupboards and sharing drinks from the cabinet like naughty teenagers. How I, within a week, had gone from a well-respected, married man with a good local reputation and people who regarded me as their son, to this isolated pariah was hard to fathom. It had been just over a week since I had left the village and here I was 'in splendid isolation,' but there was no joy in these circumstances.

I kept checking my phone to see if Misty had left a message recording her safe arrival, but none arrived. Out of nowhere, now unprotected by her concern, I felt a wave of grief for the loss of Katie, whose infuriating instructions had been my way of life. Everything familiar had been removed, and I was now without context. I did not want to remain here another night. I rang my aunt and asked if I could stay for a couple of days.

"Oh, yes, dear," she said. "We'll be a bit cramped, but you're always welcome."

I realised she was the last person on this earth who would still say that. With everyone else, I had destroyed my reputation or been forgotten. I was not good at staying in touch.

My aunt listened quietly as I told her.

"You're in a pickle, and no mistake," she said.

It was almost impossible to imagine her as being related to my father, but she was. One cousin remained in the house, but her two brothers had left. Being female, I suppose, she viewed me as guilty, but family, and somehow let me off. I told them the whole story, because I had nothing left to protect.

I stayed there for a week, and my aunt talked about her childhood, and the beatings my dad had got from his father, and the uncertainties, but how she was always a princess in her daddy's eyes. How behavioural whims can shape a life. Perhaps it explained a bit, but I was largely beyond caring.

I heard no news from Misty. Not a jot. I scanned her local paper on the internet and sometimes saw a person I knew mentioned in the news in that small way that local papers do. A client I had had remarked that "the flower show was the best they could remember," and the comment was quoted beside a photograph. I studied it more than once as if it might explain something. I read other papers too, but nothing happened which could lift me from my depression.

I determined that very day to get myself a life and told my aunt that I would look for lodging nearby. She seemed pleased, in the sense that it might mean I was stirring myself to face the future. It had only been a week and two weeks since the whole episode began, but it seemed forever.

Soon, I had some place in a suburb with facilities. Nothing special anymore. Left to myself, I was not a showy man, and I had no one to show off to. I got some kind of job, doing books for the small clients of a solicitor and kept myself to myself. No one called or rang apart from my aunt, who alone, along with my cousin remained interested in my existence. I had no reason to go out, apart from work, and unlike Bernard, could not lose myself in films or a lady paid to show me some attention.

Having so recently been dazzled by a love I had considered beyond the possible, imitations offered no relief. I kept asking myself how a girl could love a man so much that she would travel half way across the world to see him, and then drop him without compunction to take up with the man sent to keep her safe. Was it because she saw qualities in me, or just that she was whimsically changeable? I had no idea, but I loved her nonetheless.

How she could give her untouched body to mine, and show rapture without protection or regard for her own safety. It was that crazy headstrong abandon in her, suddenly revealed, which had destroyed the last vestiges of control in my behaviour. She gave me everything a man could desire, but now it seemed to have been on loan. The hours had stretched into days and then two weeks and still no word. I received a letter from Katie's solicitor saying she was seeking a divorce 'on the grounds of my unreasonable behaviour' and making an unsettling reference to my inheritance. Knowing Katie, that was not unsurprising, but I thought to hire a solicitor of my own. His advice gave no room for cheer, and I readied myself for fresh deprivations.

In Australia, Bernard had reached an emotional plateau and no longer sought for meetings with Ruby or any other replacement. He sat dry-eyed through rom-coms and applied himself to the piano with renewed belief. He had no idea why. With the help of a man he met through work, he put his lament for Misty on YouTube and waited to see if anything happened, and then suddenly, things began to change.

Following the debacle with Misty he had seen no more of Derek. However you spun it, he could not pretend his friend had acted as good friends do, and finally, after years of ridicule, he felt worth more than that. Derek rang, of course, but Bernard made sure he was always busy until the calls became infrequent. Derek was so used to 'people getting him wrong' that it is hard to imagine him losing any sleep over the matter, or admitting it if he did.

It may be true that if a man has nothing left to hang onto, he begins to discover himself, but for whatever reason, Bernard had fresh energy. Fate, the trees, or some divine influence sometime seem to smile on us, and so with him. Life began to change. His phone rang one day, and it was Samantha, Derek's girlfriend, now his ex, who asked if they could meet in town. Bernard felt a warmth, which had recently been absent from his life. It was some time since anyone had paid him sincere attention, and he agreed to meet her the next evening.

I cannot really explain the events, but suffice it to say, Samantha had grown tired of Derek's pyrotechnics and called it a day. When she spoke to Bernard, she told him that Derek apparently was now hooked up with some air hostess who was happy to receive his brand of charm. Samantha found it all amusing, and it was clear she had risked no emotional capital with his unlamented friend. When they met, initially for a drink, the evening stretched into a meal and long conversations. She seemed genuinely pleased to be with him, though Bernard was unsure of the reason. His new confidence and self-knowledge were more attractive than he realised, and his talents had taken on a sharper edge.

He found she sought his advice on varied matters, and freed from the need to impress, his comments were regarded as valuable. She believed in him, and that was a new experience to enjoy. Confidence begets confidence, they say, and gradually his began to grow. She tuned his marketing efforts with practised skill, and his YouTube publications started to attract a level of interest.

Compliments were paid, and girls, who would have made him gawp in his previous life, left comments on his music such as, "This is beautiful. It is as though you read my mind," "What an amazing talent," and, "Who is this guy?"

Initially Bernard was dazzled by the remarks, but Samantha reminded him that people feel free to praise if no money is involved. Despite her caution she seemed pleased, and even proud, and the numbers kept on creeping up. In part she felt she had discovered him, and then some music man mentioned him, and all hell broke loose. Or do I mean heaven? Record companies approached him. This long neglected man could hardly understand his progress, but Samantha watched his back. He gave her what no one else could: perspective without self-interest. That had always been Bernard's way, to talk as though he was invisible and only the situation should be noticed. At last, he, himself, was in the circle of significance, and Samantha helped him manage the change.

How strange it was that Misty, without meaning to, had fanned the flames of his old innocence, which, welded to a new maturity, gave him a voice which demanded recognition. Friends in the right places – and Samantha had a few – fanned the interest, and his life seemed changed forever.

In kissing Samantha, he felt himself at home. With her he always told the truth, and never sought to impress her. She liked him for what he was, and not what he had, which we know is not unusual. That had happened by accident, and Derek – the man who made it happen – was no doubt shaking his head.

Out of the blue, in one of the trash papers I had started looking at, because gossip seemed to divert me from my grief, I read about a new YouTube sensation and there, unbelievably, was a picture of Bernard with some attractive woman described as his girlfriend, Samantha. Apparently he had put that song onto the net, and some influential man had come across it. The rest was fame as people say. I couldn't help but smile. There was no doubt that he deserved his break, and suddenly his bald head looked quite distinguished. Fame, it seems, can alter our perception of a man.

Samantha was smiling at him as though he was the coming sage.

~2~

Back in the village, when Misty walked through the door alone, her mum and dad just hugged her at the beginning and asked her if she was alright. They acted as if she had been somehow seduced, and I had plotted her downfall all along. She felt bad, of course, about the way she had left me on my own with little announcement, but the meeting with Bernard had disturbed her, and the email to me was so fierce and final in its tone that she could not see how we might continue. She was not proud of herself, but a future without her mother and father was not possible, and if I was the price she had to pay, then so be it. Ruthless it may have been, and possibly impulsive, but it was adult in its reasoning, and that was a new departure for this girl. Despite their curiosity they let Misty go to her room and recover from the journey. They had lots of questions, naturally, but they would have to wait. At least she was safe.

There is a quality about people who are innocent which cannot, I think, be imitated. Misty had been attacked and mauled at in the cinema, but she had never let herself be open to a man in the way she had with me. Among her friends and community, she had a place as a quietish, almost scholarly girl, naive about much of life. She was more knowing than her reputation allowed, but it was an academic knowingness. In hard terms she had done very little apart from move around in safe circles doing safe things. She had not done drugs, or drunk herself to within a glass's width of oblivion, snogged boys behind the bus shelter, or stayed out all night at raves. This was not her interest or her style. It is part of the reason why David was so protective of her and went to such lengths to ensure that nothing awkward happened on her trip.

We might say he moulded the girl he sheltered, but with Katie's help, and her own curiosity, she had begun to test the boundaries protecting her from a more open life some time before she got on that plane. In the morning when she awoke, her parents knew better than to ask too many questions.

The previous night, when they lay in bed, Margaret had told David before they slept, "She'll tell us when she's ready," and so they hoped.

She was their daughter, but now more guarded and wary, as if her acceptance in the house was not automatic. The reason became clear when Margaret suggested they go up and see Katie and the Sadler's.

"Might as well get it over with," said Margaret, and David nodded silently.

He was more the passenger in this case, full of anger at me of course, but not of subtlety. He kept asking himself how he had trusted such a plastic man. Misty would stare at her phone quite often, but it remained silent. Perhaps she was wondering if I would message her as I was wondering the same thing in reverse: a classic case of 'manners' versus communication.

Later in the morning, they set off to see the Sadlers. Misty felt nervous, which was understandable but had no choice in the matter – villages and families being what they are – and within ten minutes, they pulled up outside the door. When it opened, it was Geoff who answered it. A small relief. Of everyone involved, he was the least eccentric and the most reasonable.

"Come in, come in," he said, as if it was an ordinary visit, and they all shuffled into the living room. There on the coach lay Katie with her leg in plaster, and her mother sitting on a chair nearby. There was an atmosphere.

"Bitch," said Katie. Perhaps not the perfect start, and both men moved to calm the room before events got out of hand.

"I don't think it was entirely Misty's fault," said Sandra, or Mrs. Ballard as I still thought of her, but Katie was not to be robbed of her moment of hysteria. "She knew what she was doing."

Katie, it was clear, had a larger appetite for melodrama than compromise, and no one around her was sure how to react.

"We all make mistakes" said David, and Geoff, attempting to be helpful, added that Misty was not the first person in this room to have had an affair, and to be forgiven. His wife stiffened at the reference, but she decided they would continue that discussion later in the day.

Margaret, always the cooler one, saw things would soon get out of hand making a bad situation worse and said, "I think we'll come back when things get calmer."

But as they left, Katie shouted, "I hope you die."

Throughout this exchange, Misty remained strangely detached and watched events without speaking. Her pale cheeks were her only commentary. Like many people *in extremis*, she became an observer of her situation rather than a manager and was clearly withdrawing deeper and deeper into herself. David and Margaret, unsettled by the change, sought to shield her as best they could, but was that a possibility?

Who can say what her thoughts were, but for some, she had morphed from princess to villainess in one week. Katie felt sure that she must have harboured designs on me long before we left for Australia, but I still think that to be unlikely. In her demented and hysteric state, she could almost believe her cousin had somehow engineered her falling down the stairs. Who was to say, thought Katie, that Misty and I had not already exchanged fumbled kisses at some time before we left. Her imagination was nothing if not vigorous, and scenarios of darkening import flocked through her mind. Now squarely the centre of attention, she unconsciously milked her genuine feelings to engage the maximum sympathy from her relatives. Once she was free to move through the town, who knows the damage she might inflict. Mercy, she always felt, was a quality used only by the weak.

The mood was sombre in the car, and Margaret sat in the back so she could comfort Misty, who was not crying, but was ever more withdrawn and non-committal. It was quite clear she had not realised how badly things might appear, or that Katie would be so aggressive. It was clear that, in Australia, she had understood very little, and she was now cursing her own stupidity.

Over the coming days, as she walked through the village, or along the breakwater, mimicking my routine when under stress, she realised at each turn that she was looked at in a different way. No one spoke directly to her face, but that quality of indulgence, which had always marked her relations with the community, seemed to have been lost and replaced by a more guarded or sometimes teasing courtesy. Not everyone was kind, and some even welcomed her downfall. She had become part stranger in her hometown, and the experience was unpleasant. More than that, it was like being pilloried, and she had no answer to her predicament. Her mother and father tried to reassure her, but she could sense that even they were not sure how much they understood about events when she was overseas. She did not seek to explain herself. Their uncertainty was less bruising than a judgement would have been, so she remained and was left in a world of cruel ambivalence.

Geoff and David met for a pint and discussed the matter. Neither of them apportioned any blame to Misty. The blame fell squarely on me. Apparently, I had received a decent inheritance from my father, and it had turned my head.

"Money is the root," said David sipping at his beer, and

Geoff agreed. It did not help that they had always liked me, and could not understand how I had changed so much. Only one boy seemed cheered by the news. That lad who had approached her at the sweet corn festival saw an opportunity to get a little closer to a girl who had brushed him off so professionally at that event. He managed to bump into her and ask her where she was going. Starved of friendship and understanding, she was more open to his approach, and soon they were setting off on a walk along the cliffs. Cheery he may have been, but he was also canny, and he believed in letting the fish have a good taste of the bait before tugging the line. He made no move to touch her on the walk and played the perfect gentleman.

Over the following week, they met three more times, and you might say, he was her only friend. She had resisted all efforts to go back to Katie's and 'clear the air.' That was not going to happen any time soon, in her opinion. She had only gone on the first visit out of goodwill toward her parents, but the outcome had not surprised her. Her thoughts were full of me, as mine were of her, but for obscure reasons, neither of us rang or texted the other.

Sometimes I entered the words "Are you OK? xxx" into the phone, but I never sent them.

I was not sure if she was still at that stage when she thought life was a tasting menu and not a meal; that her whirlwind romance with me had been an experience but not a commitment. I was filled with a curious diffidence and uncertainty about her position. You can probably guess my dialogue with myself.

"Did she really love me?"

"Was her attention to me just an expression of her disappointment with Bernard?"

"Did she have any deep feelings?"

I loved her, and she filled my thoughts, but I was not used to being the centre of someone else's attention. It seemed more than possible that it had been a glance rather than a serious change of view. Had it now moved from me to some other beau? I had no idea. I buried myself, as far as was possible, in my nondescript professional responsibilities and in socialising with my aunt who did not know me that well but was a women with a naturally sympathetic ear whose manner was very different to her brother's. Needless to say, they had not been close and she did not seem to mourn him.

Misty and the cheery lad were not getting any closer in the emotional sense. She was too preoccupied with her circumstances, and he with her looks for anything deeper to develop between them, but for their different reasons they spent more time together. Her mother and father, of course, were aware of the connection, but only commented about it between themselves. For the moment, they were not sure of her or how she thought. The girl they knew and loved had left them a short time before and returned, it seemed, changed beyond all understanding. Whatever they said publicly, or tried to think, they were not totally unaware that Misty herself may have helped orchestrate her love affair with me. They reserved their ministrations to providing meals and shelter. They were really at a loss as how to proceed.

After a few walks, he moved to kiss her, and she allowed his lips to briefly touch her cheek, but really there was nothing there to move them, apart from lust, and she did not share his. It was a barren experience for her and, if anything, made her sad. Once again, it was a kiss born more of custom than intent, and he managed to laugh off his actions. He was just having fun, if truth be told, and knew no one else in the town apart from a couple of casual drinking mates, so he would bide his time and wait till she became more receptive.

I don't know when it was that I decided to hire a car and drive down there so I could see how she was, and if she was alone. Looking back, it was a mad idea, but I was not really in the mood to be sensible. I decided to go down on the Saturday when I would not interfere with work. The journey was about four hours and not uncomfortable. If needs must, I could easily hire a room, and if needs were not must, I would just return later in that day. I would be tired, but what else could I do? I drove in silence without the radio. I had enough thoughts in my head to pass the time without some announcer or singer interrupting them. The car droned on and on, as did my constant examining of events but without resolution.

I could not forget how passionate she was, or how she had given herself to me without protection and with abandon. The look in her eye when I entered her, her manner of squeezing against me when I was considered to have said something funny. How she sang my praises all the time and made those thoughtful remarks about my character. It had been a period of undiluted bliss.

People use that term casually, but I had experienced it with my darling. I admitted to myself that much of my conduct was questionable if looked at starkly and without sentiment, but I know of few people who would have resisted such an onslaught. It was clear that Misty, herself, was overwhelmed by events. The disturbing performance from Bernard, who I had thought to be a figure of ridicule, before he revealed his impressive inner being, and the anger of her parents had made her think about us again, permanently or not, I had no idea.

Could it be, I prayed, that she would use that sweet and delicate charm of hers to persuade them I really was the man they thought I was before we left, and that we had been powerless to resist a love which was stronger than us both. Even I, at some twelve years older than her, had my fears that David and Margaret might not subscribe to that theory, but I still hoped. As I approached the village, descending down the winding road from the hills which surrounded it, I was caught up in the familiar view of the buildings I had grown to love and the sea beyond them: blue and calm. It was a beautiful day and everything looked like some untouched picture whose purity I hoped my presence would not disturb. I parked a bit above the harbour and sat in the car looking at the walls and the breakwater which jutted out into the sea from it, a beautiful grey granite structure which had resisted many gales. The irony was not lost on me.

Looking around, I saw a couple on a bench with the man's arm around the women. As I got used to the light I recognised them both. It was the cheery chap from David's party and Misty. How could this be? I just sat there looking at them, and then he seemed to turn and kiss her. The chances of my being there to witness that were not measurable, and it seemed a cruel fate which had allowed me to see it.

I did not get out of the car but just sat there looking at them. The kiss, when it happened, was brief and perfunctory, but still she had allowed it. Did I need to see anything else? No, but still I sat there with my head and heart churning in the seat of this rented car, parked in a village from which I now felt exiled. I have never felt so lonely or so desolate. The girl for whom I had sacrificed everything was succumbing to another man's advances with casual abandon, and all I could do was watch. My Misty, my sweet and darling Misty, had stepped on my hopes with hardly a backward glance, and I could not understand it.

I started the car, turned round, and then drove off. I must have been there no more than half an hour, and I had no wish to die on the way back, but it was almost impossible to concentrate. Finally, once I was far from town, I stopped the car and allowed the tears to fall. Might there be an explanation? A fool will clutch at any straws, but it seemed to me that, like a mermaid, she had beckoned me towards her and charmed me to my ruin. I loved her with all my heart and my sense of desolation felt unlimited. I longed to turn and ask her why or how, but I could not. I am not a man given to anger, so all I felt was an overwhelming sadness and a sense of loss. In the fortnight since I had seen her, more must have happened than I could imagine, but I could not begin to piece together the events which might lead from our rapturous union to that kiss in the harbour.

Finally, I started the car and drove again until I reached the place I called home because I slept there. It had no memories. I had no one to speak to and nothing to hang onto apart from the well-meaning attentions of my aunt, whose views on my life I did not seek. I could only speculate how odd my circumstances and recent life must have seemed.

After three weeks of total silence, I was adjusting to my lot, and rebuilding some routine. I ate a meal at some café in the evening, and lunched on something simple at the office. I had no friends to speak to, but no doubt, that would come in time. Fitting in was my speciality, after all. One evening, as I was sitting in my rooms watching a stupid film where girls still kissed boys and people sat on fair rides half their life, the door-bell rang. I presumed it was my cousin come to chat. She did that sometimes, out of sympathy.

I opened the door, and there was Misty with a suitcase in her hand. Not the Misty that I knew, but some new, haunted figure, unsure, uncertain, and adrift. Her visit had affected her, that much was clear, but was it permanently.

You know what I'm like with drowning and troubled figures. You remember Katie in the doorway when we met. I looked at her and she stared back at me. I took her suitcase from her hand. He eyes seemed full of a rawness born of grief or loss or some emotion not yet understood. That may have been my imagination, but there was some profound change about her.

She opened her mouth and said, "You are a good man."

I stared at her in shock, uncertain how to respond, and then I thought.

"A good man. Is that all I am?"

I had got the girl, but had I got the dream?

ABOUT THE AUTHOR

Peter Wells, who has lived by the maxim," If you can meet with triumph and disaster, and treat those two imposters just the same" has had a life, working in the corporate, financial and self-employed worlds, and in his spare time has enjoyed adventures on a number of continents and sailing over several seas.

His writing is inspired by his working and traveling life, and the people he has met through them. He now lives just south of London and is the proud father of three daughters.